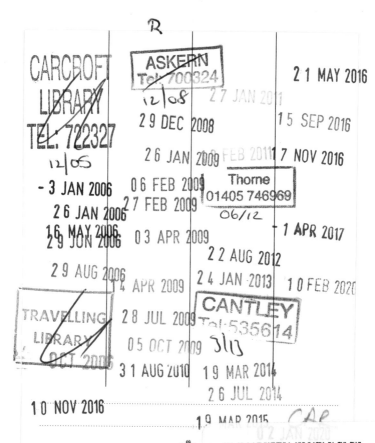

R

CARCROFT
LIBRARY
TEL: 722327
12/05

- 3 JAN 2006
2 6 JAN 2006
1 6 MAY 2006
2 9 JUN 2006

2 9 AUG 2006

TRAVELLING
LIBRARY
OCT 2006

ASKERN
Tel: 700324
12/08
2 9 DEC 2008

2 6 JAN 2009

06 FEB 2009
2 7 FEB 2009

03 APR 2009

1 4 APR 2009

2 8 JUL 2009

05 OCT 2009

3 1 AUG 2010

2 7 JAN 2011

1 7 FEB 2011

Thorne
01405 746969
06/12

2 2 AUG 2012

2 4 JAN 2013

CANTLEY
Tel: 535614
5/13

1 9 MAR 2014

2 6 JUL 2014

1 9 MAR 2015

2 1 MAY 2016

1 5 SEP 2016

1 7 NOV 2016

- 1 APR 2017

1 0 FEB 2020

1 0 NOV 2016

0 2 JAN 2020

CAP

Doncaster
Metropolitan Borough

DONCASTER LIBRARY AND INFORMATION SERVICES

Please return/renew this item by the last date shown.
Thank you for using your library.

D1610095

Nemesis Trail

Before it started to lose its name and soul to a man named Durgan Vosper, Harper's Mill was a lively logging town. Now, decent folk are forced to run and hide as mayhem and murder stalk the streets.

When Rick Jarrett drifts into town he's mistaken for another of Vosper's gunmen, but he's a man on a mission. Looking for answers to questions that no other man dares to ask, Jarrett won't quit until he knows the truth – or is six foot under.

For this he's willing to lay his life and his love on the line. That's the price a man must pay when he's riding the Nemesis Trail.

Nemesis Trail

Eugene Clifton

A Black Horse Western

ROBERT HALE · LONDON

© Eugene Clifton 2005
First published in Great Britain 2005

ISBN 0 7090 7831 5

Robert Hale Limited
Clerkenwell House
Clerkenwell Green
London EC1R 0HT

Typeset by
Derek Doyle & Associates, Shaw Heath.
Printed and bound in Great Britain by
Antony Rowe Limited, Wiltshire

CHAPTER ONE

Flames shot into the sky above the town known as Harper's Mill. The fire raged through tinder-dry shingles and by the time the townsfolk gathered the back of the church was blazing. Men ran to fetch buckets and form a chain from the waterfront, while young Ged Dwyer, the saddler's son, ran up the hill to the minister's house.

After the dry summer the river was low and Grant Pechey from the telegraph office stood with his feet anchored in mud, knee deep so he could reach the water, swinging the filled buckets to José Ferraro, who'd run out still wearing his apron, the customers in his cantina forgotten. José was a man of God and he loved the little church; he'd helped to fix those shingles which were now burning so fiercely.

Passed to Sam Dwyer and Bert Henderson the storekeeper and through another half dozen pairs of hands the water slopped, eventually being tossed into the fire by young Harve Butcher. Another chain formed alongside the first, women and children passing the empty buckets back to the river.

Ferraro glared up at the scattering of white clouds. 'We need rain.' Swooping and lifting Pechey didn't have the breath to agree.

Father Martin wasn't an early riser. He'd been known to

sleep soundly until noon through the ear-splitting din of log sleds rolling down the road towards the river only a foot from his door; on Sundays and feast days he paid Ged Dwyer to roust him out in time for the first service. Coming to the little cabin the boy flung open the door and rushed inside. In the two years since Father Martin's arrival he'd lost his fear of the man in black and he went in yelling, skidding across the room into the cubby-hole where the minister slept.

Once he was awake the clergyman moved fast. A big man of some thirty summers, he crashed into the wall as he struggled to pull a cassock over his night-shirt for the sake of modesty. Ged reached up to help him, dragging the black cloth down over the short blunt stump of the priest's right arm, steering him through the doorway.

'Looks like it's got quite a hold.' Chalky White came from the livery stable and fell into step alongside the minister, taking two hurried strides to Father Martin's one, rubbing a hand over his face in an attempt to clear the stale whiskey from his system. 'Ged, go back to my yard, you'll find more buckets by the feed bins.'

Every man, woman and child was out watching the fire. Lily Godine and the girls who worked for her above stairs at the Double Eagle broke the habit of a lifetime by appearing on the street before midday, most of them coming out without benefit of paint or powder. A redhead called Tabitha even joined the line, passing empty buckets to the little girl who swept up at the saloon, both of them ignoring the disapproving glances of the town's respectable matrons. Alongside Lily Godine and the rest of her girls were a score of workers from the sawmill, shouting encouragement to the fire-fighters or the flames as the mood took them and making more noise than the congregation ever achieved in praise of the Lord on a Sunday morning.

Seeing where the need was greatest Father Martin went to relieve Grant Pechey, his powerful left hand effortlessly raising full buckets and swinging them into José's grasp, working so furiously he was soon splashed from head to foot. For a few minutes it seemed they might win the fight as more water was thrown onto the fire.

Built to be seen from the river, the church stood like a monument at the bottom of Main Street, not far from the wharf and the sawmill. Suddenly the breeze that feathered the water with little waves strengthened, gusting to send sparks up towards the buildings on the corner opposite the Double Eagle saloon.

For a few precious minutes the firefighters had to concentrate their efforts on damping down the roofs of the saddler's shop and Ferraro's cantina. Unchecked, the fire in the church crept further along the walls and across the shingles, the brisk crackle of flame growing louder, the fire so hot that there was very little smoke.

Everyone was too busy to notice the fashionable ebony rig pulled by matching black horses racing past the sawmill and onto the river front. It appeared through the heat haze as if it had been driven from the bowels of hell. Along the bucket chain voices were hushed and the workers paused to stare. The carriage was driven by a man whose clothes were as sombre as those of Father Martin, though they bore no resemblance to the minister's plain coarse cloth.

Durgan Vosper was around thirty years old, distinguished in a black silk shirt and a suit of fine European wool. His boots were soft black leather, even the heels tooled and highly polished. Light from the flames glittered dimly in the jet beads that decorated his hat band.

The matched black Arabians sidled uneasily, unsettled by the fire. Their owner's small hands subdued them with easy expertise and they stood with nostrils flared and eyes rolling up to show the whites. From the bunch of four riders behind the carriage a man with the flat brown face of a South American Indian jumped down to hold the horses' heads.

'Good morning, Father,' Vosper called. 'You seem to have a problem.'

Sweat pouring down his face the minister relinquished his post to Sam Dwyer and stepped out of the river mud and back onto solid ground. 'Hardly a good morning, Mr Vosper. You and your men wouldn't know how the fire started, I suppose?'

Vosper laughed, beckoning to one of the men still on horseback, a tall gangly figure with long dark hair showing under his Stetson and a badge pinned to his waistcoat. 'What do you think, Bergquist? Surely the father's sermons would be enough to deter anyone from setting light to the church?'

Bergquist shrugged. 'Never heard a one of 'em,' he said, his voice deep and rasping. 'Most likely somebody got careless with a candle.'

'In that case this might be classed as an act of God,' Vosper said. His eyes, almost as dark as the clothes he wore, reflected an unholy red glow from the flames. 'A demonstration of the good Lord's wrath or a warning to the sinners amongst us. There should be a great increase in your congregation after this, Father, though regrettably they'll have to gather out of doors.'

Father Martin's brows drew together, the fingers of his left hand clenching into a fist. He sucked in a long deep breath. 'The church may be past saving, but until it's rebuilt I'll go on holding services wherever I can.'

He glanced across the street where two men had appeared at the door of the cantina. One of them was huge, having to duck to pass through the doorway. He wiped his mouth on his sleeve as he came, then picked food out from between yellow teeth with a filthy finger-nail. The other man was small, barely reaching the giant's elbow, but there was a malevolence about his narrow face and dark eyes that prevented him from looking insignificant beside his gigantic companion. 'I'm sure you'll tell me Brossman and his friend Felipe weren't passing by the church early this morning?'

Vosper shrugged. 'Who knows? All my men come and go as they please except when I have work for them. But you don't need to worry, Father, I'll be happy to provide timber for a new church, there's plenty of space up above the town. It seems I'm to have this plot for my new mill after all, since God has obviously finished with it.'

'The church has stood here since Audie Harper built his mill and laid out the town,' Father Martin replied. 'I see no reason to move it.'

Vosper went on as if the minister hadn't spoken. 'I favour the northern side of the valley. A church built there will command a good view of the river and there would be no disturbance caused by noise from the mill. We could provide a small dwelling for you at the same time.'

'Harper gave this land to the church,' Father Martin said stubbornly, raising his voice so it could be heard over the roar of the fire.

With a sigh Vosper dragged on the reins to still his restive team. 'But Harper is dead. Times change, it's a wise man who knows it.' He turned to Bergquist. 'I think you'd better remove these people to a safe distance, Marshal. When the last of those timbers burn through the church may collapse. I'm sure you'll agree we don't want anyone hurt, Father.' With a flourish of the whip Vosper turned the carriage, nodding to Brossman and Felipe before he drove the Arabians up the sloping street.

There was no hope of saving the little building. With some reluctance the buckets were abandoned and the flames licked their way greedily towards the front porch. The marshal ushered the townsfolk towards the wharf. A few refused to retreat, a small knot of them gathering in front of the Double Eagle hotel to watch the fire burn itself out. Only Father Martin remained by the blazing ruin.

'Tough luck,' Brossman said, a grin on his heavy featured face as he came to stand beside the minister. 'Don't reckon anyone's bin listenin' to your prayers.'

'On the contrary,' Father Martin said. 'All that we say is heard and all that we do is seen, whether it's for good or evil. One day you'll see the truth of that, Brossman.'

'An' me, you think I am a sinner?' The little man beside Brossman hunched his shoulders beneath the filthy poncho he wore, his lips twisting in a humourless smile. 'Maybe you think we had somethin' to do with this fire, eh?'

Father Martin didn't reply.

'You're a special man, eh Padre?' Felipe persisted. 'He watches over you, this God of yours?'

'He's a friend to everyone, He doesn't have favourites.'

'But you, you spend all your time talkin' to Him, eh? You're a good man.' The little black eyes had an unholy light in them. 'Like a saint, yes? He don't want you to have a hard time.'

'Yeah,' Brossman said. 'Shame you an' Him couldn't stop the church burnin' down, that would have been a real live miracle.'

'Maybe there's still time.' The little man's hand appeared from beneath the begrimed woollen blanket. The object he held gleamed, reflecting the glare from the flames. He offered it to Brossman. 'This little statue, it can do a miracle, eh?'

Father Martin's eyes widened as he recognized the small shiny thing that passed between them. 'You took that when you started the fire.'

Brossman looked hurt. 'No, me an' Felipe came by here on our way to the cantina an' we saw the smoke. We went into the church to make sure nobody was in there an' we noticed that purty thing settin' on the table. Figured it was a real pity to let it burn. But seein' as how you an' God got this special arrangement, reckon you can just walk right in there an' fetch it out without gettin' hurt, ain't that right?' He looked down at the minister's bare feet and grinned. 'Can't be no harder than walkin' on water.'

The minister made a grab for the crucifix but Brossman brushed him aside and swung his arm to toss the golden image into the church porch. It lay close up against the burning wooden wall, its bright surface reflecting the flickering glow from the flames.

From among the gathered townsfolk came shouts of dismay as Father Martin headed for the fire. He seemed not to hear their warnings. The black clad figure raced towards the inferno, his one hand lifted to shelter his face from the blast of heat, the long skirts of his cassock flapping as he ran. The front of the church had been the last to catch light but as the priest approached the roof creaked ominously.

'No! Father!' José Ferraro pushed past Bergquist, starting forward to follow the priest. The marshal's long arm reached out to pluck him back. Flames had begun to eat into the porch and the solid wooden door, creating a deadly arc of fire. The dry timber spat and crackled in the ferocious heat and the watchers held their breath, not understanding what their priest was doing. Apart from Father Martin only Felipe moved, edging closer as if to watch, his tongue flicking out to moisten hot dry lips, eyes narrowed in concentration.

Though bright scraps of burning wood rained down around Father Martin and landed on his hair and clothes

11

they didn't ignite, quenched perhaps by the soaking he'd got as he'd stood in the river, though wisps of smoke began to rise from his robe. He swooped towards the golden crucifix, his powerful left arm outstretched. There was a muted crack, perhaps the sound of a roof beam giving way somewhere in the heart of the church.

Inexplicably the priest stumbled. Twisting as if in an attempt to keep his footing, Father Martin lurched against the blazing wall to one side of the porch. Nothing but charcoal and ash, it collapsed under his weight. With a great roar and a sigh that might have come from the throats of all the angels in heaven, the blaze flared afresh to devour this new offering, flames shooting up as if reaching for the clear blue sky above. A wail of anguish rose from those who watched but the priest made no sound, nor did his body stir again as cloth and flesh began to shrivel.

CHAPTER TWO

It was cold in the forest, the sort of cold that could steal a man's toes or fingers without him even noticing. Rick Jarrett climbed stiffly out of the saddle. Putting his feet down carefully because he couldn't feel them, he stomped around on the frozen ground until his toes began to hurt. Then he walked, the scrawny bay in its tattered winter coat trailing after him. The horse favoured its near hind leg and Jarrett didn't object when it paused to nuzzle aside the snow and snatch a meagre mouthful of yellowed grass; they were working their way up to the top of a high ridge and it wasn't easy going. Above the trees there was blue sky. As the sun rose it would warm the air but in the shade of the tall ponderosa pines the thaw had barely started.

The trees thinned a little and finally Jarrett stepped out onto a bare rocky ledge. A whole world lay at his feet. It was maybe three thousand feet down to the river, a wide winding ribbon of ice that shone silver in the sun. From somewhere below in the depths of the forest the sound of axes biting into wood and trees falling blended with the muffled shouts of men. The noise echoed from the surrounding hills and beneath the thick cover of dark green only a couple of thin columns of smoke showed where the logging camp lay.

Far away more smoke rose from a cluster of buildings at

the riverside, no bigger than a scattering of thrown seeds at this distance. The only visible trail angled down to the right towards the logging camp and Jarrett pulled the horse's head around and urged it into motion. The sounds grew louder as he descended, until he could clearly hear the clank of chains and the lowing of oxen and, once, the piercing neigh of a horse.

The trail levelled some and Jarrett lifted back into the saddle. A slight breeze fluttered the pines and the smell hit him. He was back in the land of men. After weeks travelling alone his nose wrinkled at the stink of humanity; he'd grown too accustomed to the powerful odour of the furs he wore to notice that he didn't smell any too sweet himself.

The sounds stopped. Peace shrouded the forest, but it was an unsettling silence. Jarrett drew the Winchester from its saddle holster, dragging off the rags that protected it from the damp cold. He worked a round into the chamber and rode on, ears and eyes alert to any sound or movement. Minutes passed, five, ten, and still that uncanny quiet stretched out before him; he'd have thought he was deaf but for the muffled beat of his horse's hoofs thudding on the hard packed snow.

Catching his mood the horse was jittery and when the silence finally broke the bay spun round in the taking of a breath, ready to run. A primeval scream flew echoing to the hills, blending into the great crashing wave of sound that followed. Men shouted and cheered and a volley of shots tore skywards, ripping into the branches high above. Mastering the trembling horse Jarrett pushed it to a lope, heading towards the din. A few words shouted louder than the rest began to make sense and as he rode out into the clearing he knew what he was going to see.

The mob had already chosen their tree, though pines don't lend themselves too well to a hanging. A rope had been flung over a bough that was deemed long enough and strong enough to hold the victim's weight, and they were heaving him towards it, a couple of dozen lumber-men all trying to get a hand on him at once. The condemned man was doing his best to resist, digging in his heels, trying to wriggle free, but he hadn't a hope. As Jarrett angled towards the lynch mob a tall skinny figure stepped out of the crowd, one hand raised in greeting.

'If you was thinkin' of interferin', mister, I'd advise against it.' The man's voice rattled like a handful of loose gravel. He had long hair hanging lank beneath a brown Stetson and as he pulled his coat open to display the badge pinned on his vest he smiled. The expression didn't look as if it came easy to the hard thin face.

'What did he do?' Jarrett asked, his eyes on the strug-gling figure. With his mouth wide open the man looked as if he was shouting but Jarrett could hear nothing over the yells of the rabble. The loggers had his neck in the noose now and were fighting for the privilege of heaving on the other end of the rope.

'Stole a horse.'

'Never heard of a logging camp with its own lawman.'

'I'm from Vosperville, down by the river. Name's Bergquist.' He offered a hand.

After the briefest hesitation Jarrett loosed his right hand from the Winchester long enough to grip the bony fingers. 'Rick Jarrett.'

They watched as the horse thief was heaved into the air, his legs kicking. Once he was strung up the noise from the mob subsided and the man's strangled bid for breath could be heard. His hands had been tied behind him but in his struggle he'd wrenched them free and now he was trying to get his fingers round the rope where it bit into his neck. It was already too tight and he scrabbled uselessly at his flesh, his fingernails drawing blood. Pathetic

15

mewing sounds escaped from his lips as his face darkened. Giving up his attempt to loosen the noose he swung a hand above his head and took a grip on the rope, heaving hard to take some of his weight.

The loggers jeered, one of them jabbing at the victim's arm with a pike pole to make him let go, but the force of the blow set the man swinging and his boot landed on a small branch lower down the tree so the pressure on his throat eased. Laughter rippled through the crowd and they surged like coyotes round a dead steer, not interfering as the man managed to take a tortured breath before he swung loose again and the rope cut deeper into his windpipe.

It was almost over. Then with a crack that reverberated around the clearing the bough gave way and the man fell sprawling to the ground. Whooping and cheering the mob descended and dragged their victim upright again, a dozen eager hands grabbing him by the arms and legs and hair, a hefty punch to the head subduing his feeble attempts to fight. This time a logger climbed up to toss the rope over a higher branch. The condemned man was begging for mercy, a torrent of words rasping from his damaged throat, but once again he was hauled aloft, his arms and legs flailing, his face contorted into a rictus of pain and terror.

A shot rang out, the sound echoing from the hills. Jarrett's bullet took the dying man just off centre, straight to the heart. The body gave a single convulsive jerk then hung limp.

There was an angry growl from the mob, and as one, the enraged loggers started towards Jarrett where he sat his horse alongside the marshal, another cartridge in the breech and the Winchester ready in his hands. 'There's no law against putting a bullet into a dead man,' Jarrett said, pitching his voice loud enough to carry.

Bergquist's thin lips turned down. 'It was a good shot,' he conceded. 'But he was still kickin', Mr Jarrett. What's the matter, you got no stomach for a hangin'?'

'I can stomach a whole lot,' Jarrett said, 'but I never did care to watch a lynch mob at work. Reckon they had their fun.'

The loggers were still coming, the man with the pike pole at the front. Bergquist stepped forward, a hand held up in appeasement. 'Time you boys got back to work,' he said. 'Vosper pays a bounty of a hundred dollars for a horse thief and you boys are due half of it, that'll pay for a few bottles of whiskey when you come into town on Saturday night.'

There was a ragged cheer from the men. Only one or two seemed inclined to argue, but with wary looks at the Winchester they slowly moved away, leaving the dead man forlorn and forgotten as he swung in the breeze.

'No hard feelin's, Mr Jarrett,' Bergquist said. 'You look like it's a while since you had a square meal. Let's go see what the shantyboys are cookin' up.'

'No thanks.' Offering a nod of farewell Jarrett twisted in the saddle, moving the horse away. 'Don't seem to have much appetite right now.'

With the camp left behind and the sounds of falling trees once more echoing through the forest, Jarrett followed frozen sledge tracks that he guessed would take him to the town on the river. With a lame horse he was travelling slow, and three hours passed before he came to the edge of the trees. He rode into brightness and the comparative warmth of the afternoon not far from the river bank. Before him stood a sizeable town.

There had once been a sign by the trail but the post had been chopped through, and the top lay drunkenly against a tree stump, the words so scarred by bullet holes that Jarrett could barely make them out. It seemed

Harper's Mill no longer announced its name to visitors. His nose wrinkled as a vile stench hit him. The carcass of a dog lay just beyond the fallen sign and it looked as if it had been there quite some time. It hadn't died of cold; there was a neat round hole in the side of its skull. The smell followed Jarrett as he rode on down the street with stores and houses to his left and a wharf jutting out into the frozen river on his right.

Ahead of him a sawmill dominated the scene, smoke belching from its chimney. The high pitched hiss of steam and the screech of metal teeth tearing through wood were uncomfortably loud to ears that had grown accustomed to the hush of the winter forest. The words 'Vosper's Sawmills' were painted in bright new lettering on the wall.

All along the river bank rough-cut lumber was heaped in rollways, waiting for the thaw. Between Jarrett and the sawmill was a level area where a start had been made on the foundations for a new building. The icy ground had been disturbed in places, showing patches of blackened soil as if there had been a fierce fire there not long ago. Under his horse's hoof metal clanked against metal and Jarrett eased the bay to a stop, staring at the black shape poking out of the half-frozen mud. He lit down, lifting the Winchester from its holster as he stepped from the saddle. When he dropped the rein the horse gave a sigh and stood resting its hind foot.

Jarrett nudged the object with the toe of his boot but it didn't come free until he kicked hard. It had once been a fancy candlestick, only fire had blackened the brass and twisted it out of shape. He bent to pick it up and as he straightened he saw two men coming out of the sawmill and heading his way.

One of them was a giant, more than a head taller than Jarrett's five foot eleven and almost as wide as he was high. The other was small and skinny, looking like a child beside his huge companion. By the colour of his skin he might have been Mexican, but there was a flatness about his features that suggested he came from further south. As he approached, his small dark eyes gazed unwinkingly at the object in Jarrett's hand.

Jarrett let the ruined candlestick fall to the ground, reading the men's faces and the way they moved, seeing nothing friendly in their intentions; big men were usually slow and of the two he judged the little Indian in the filthy blanket was the most dangerous. There was a small black-edged hole right in the centre of the blanket that had certainly been made by a bullet, and since the man was alive a fair guess suggested the slug must have been heading out, not in.

'You lookin' for somebody or just passin' through?' The giant hooked his thumbs into the wide studded belt he wore. His eyes were bright with a malevolent intelligence.

'Since you ask so politely, I'd say that's my business.' The Winchester moved in Jarrett's grasp until it was aiming at the man's right knee, his fingers poised to work the action.

The little man grinned, showing yellow teeth. 'Hey mister, you excuse my compadre, he don't have no manners. We see you ride in an' I say to my friend Brossman here, somebody should make you feel welcome, eh? Me, my name is Felipe.'

'I'm Rick Jarrett. Came here to tend to a lame horse and a powerful thirst.'

'You do both those things in Vosperville, your horse be fine here. The Double Eagle, she's a real good saloon.' The blanket the Indian wore was stiff with dirt, but it moved a little as if his hands were busy beneath. There was the faint scrape of metal on leather.

'Vosperville?' Jarrett pretended he hadn't heard the ominous noise as his brows furrowed. 'Seems I got myself lost. I thought I was on the road to Harper's Mill.' He swung round a little as if to peer at the straggle of buildings up the hill, putting himself closer to Brossman. The manoeuvre left the big man half between him and that deadly hole in the dirty woollen cloth.

'The name, it change.' Felipe's eyes were dark voids in the yellowish brown face. Despite the growing heat of the sun it seemed suddenly colder. 'Mr Vosper, he own the mill now.'

'And the town?'

'He own that too.'

'We work for Mr Vosper,' Brossman said, 'like most folk around here. This is a real quiet place, mister, an' we don't like strangers makin' trouble.'

'Well, with the welcome you two boys have given me I don't feel like a stranger.'

Jarrett's lips curved in a travesty of a smile. His head came up suddenly, his eyes widening and his mouth opening in surprise as he stared at the door of the sawmill. Brossman and Felipe both fell for the trick, turning their heads to see what had caught Jarrett's attention. Fast on his feet, a single step brought Jarrett alongside the big man so his great bulk would obscure Felipe's aim.

In the same fluid move Jarrett had the Winchester cocked and jammed under Brossman's chin, pressing the muzzle hard into his flesh. 'I appreciate you being so friendly. Only trouble is, I have an aversion to guns being pointed my way, especially when I can't see 'em. Unless you want me to give your compadre here a chance to try breathing through his neck, you might want to drop whatever you've got hidden under the blanket.'

CHAPTER THREE

Jarrett kept the rifle hard against Brossman's flesh and met Felipe's fury with a smile.

'You got a problem here, boys?' The voice sounded like metal wheels grinding over a stony street; Bergquist was back from the logging camp. He moved into view with a Colt .45 in his bony hand, its muzzle a black eye focused on Jarrett. 'You're makin' kinda free with that Winchester of yours again, mister. Reckon you got an interferin' nature.'

'I'm a peaceable man, Marshal, but like I was saying to your friends here, I don't care to have guns pointed at me.' Jarrett indicated the little Indian with the slightest tilt of his head. 'Felipe was about to show me what he's hiding under that blanket.'

Bergquist's thin face contracted in a frown but Jarrett made no move, keeping the pressure of the barrel constant against Brossman's chin. At last Bergquist nodded. 'Seems to me the man's got a point, Felipe. Maybe you've been a touch hasty.'

Scowling, the little man pushed aside the blanket with his left hand. Beneath it he wore a bandoleer adapted to carry two holsters, one of which held a pearl-handled pistol. The derringer that fitted into the other was gripped in the Indian's dirty paw, and it was aiming at Jarrett's head.

'Between the two of you it looks like you can kill me twice over,' Jarrett said, 'but that won't make Brossman here any less dead. Far as I know I've got no argument with either one of you.' His eyes didn't waver as Bergquist glanced up the street, yet he too was aware of the horsemen turning the corner by the livery stables and there was a redheaded woman in a torn lace chemise leaning from an upstairs window in the Double Eagle hotel who was watching them with interest.

'Figure Felipe was jumping the gun,' Bergquist said, holstering his Colt. 'See, we've been warned there's a killer got loose from the state prison. When a stranger rides in lookin' like he's been a long time without a decent meal or a shave it makes a man suspicious. This ain't him, Felipe, not unless he's found a way to grow six inches.'

Jarrett caught Felipe's surprise at the marshal's story but the little man recovered quickly. Showing discoloured teeth in his yellow ochre face he slid the derringer out of sight. 'Gringos, they all look the same to me.'

Lowering the Winchester, Jarrett stepped away from Brossman. The big man's face was red, but whether with anger or from holding his breath Jarrett didn't speculate; he watched and waited, ready to duck and come up fighting.

As if the same thought had crossed Bergquist's mind he took a long stride to bring himself between them. 'Guess you boys must have work to do,' he said. A growl issued from Brossman and he swivelled his head like a baited bear, but he held his peace, with the promise of another encounter in the malevolent look he gave Jarrett before he turned away.

Felipe's smile widened but his dark eyes were cold. 'We have a drink together sometime, eh?'

Jarrett nodded but he didn't return the smile as the little man left; not unless he unsealed the bottle and poured for himself, he thought.

'We like a quiet life here in Vosperville,' Bergquist said. 'Be obliged if you'd remember that.' A long bony finger lifted to touch the brim of his Stetson in dismissal and he stepped across to the saloon, stopping under the window and shouting up at the girl.

'Why don't I come up there an' join you for a while, Tabby.'

'Uh uh, you know the rules, Marshal. I'll meet you downstairs and you can buy me a drink. If you're real nice to me we'll talk about what happens after that.'

Jarrett left them to their negotiations. He gathered up the bay's reins and led the horse across to the hitching rail. The inside of the Double Eagle was hazy with smoke, most of it issuing from a pipe clamped in the mouth of the dour looking barkeep, with a small contribution made by a fat man playing solitaire, a well-chewed cigar between his lips.

The smell of dead dog had travelled the length of the street and it wasn't deterred by the swing doors or masked by the tobacco fumes. Jarrett paused to let his eyes grow accustomed to the gloom. In one corner a chair was balanced precariously on two legs. A man sat in it, worn boots propped on the table alongside an empty whiskey bottle and glass, his belly hoisted towards the ceiling and his bald head resting in the angle between the two walls. It was a neat trick, all the more impressive because a low snore suggested that the man was fast asleep.

A girl-child was sweeping the floor, barefoot and skinny in a faded brown dress that was too big for her. A cloud of dark hair obscured her face as she bent to her task. Like the rest of the saloon's occupants she ignored the new arrival.

'Beer,' Jarrett said, tossing a coin onto the counter in front of the lugubrious barman, 'and a shot of whiskey.'

He drank the beer straight down, relishing the feel and the taste after weeks on the trail, then with the whiskey glass cradled in his hands he turned to lean his back against the bar.

Having finished driving his bargain with the girl upstairs, Bergquist swung in through the doors and came to stand beside Jarrett, his gaze settling for a few moments on the child with the broom as she bent to scrape at the floor, the dress hanging down to show the budding swell of breasts. He took a couple of steps towards her and licked his lips.

'Ain't ripe yet, honey.' The voice was almost as hoarse as Bergquist's but it was a deal higher. The woman who stood at the top of the stairs was big and full-breasted, her billowing curves accentuated by the tight-fitting emerald satin gown she wore. Her hair was bleached almost white and piled up in elaborate curls. In the smoke haze she might have passed for forty, but Jarrett guessed she was doing her best to hide another ten years.

'Just lookin', Lily,' Bergquist said. 'No charge for lookin'. But I'd say Melia's near enough grown up. You ain't gonna forget your promise?'

The woman gave a practised smile. 'It'll be fair and square, Marshal. Tabitha tells me you're going calling, she said to take up a bottle of wine along with the whiskey.'

Bergquist grumbled as he handed over a dollar bill to the barkeep and took the bottles from him, then he went up the stairs three at a time, elbowing aside the woman he'd addressed as Lily and brushing past a battered canvas screen at the end of the landing.

'Want to play?' The man with the cigar spoke for the first time, tilting an eyebrow at Jarrett and riffling the cards expertly. 'Any game you want.'

'No thanks.'

'Poker here most nights,' the man persisted. 'You planning to stay awhile?'

'Depends.' Jarrett turned to the barman. 'You have rooms here?' He glanced at the woman in green who'd come down the stairs and helped herself to a drink. She gave him what was supposed to be an encouraging smile.

'Without company,' he added.

'My name's Lily Godine.' She sashayed across to him. 'What's the matter, mister, afraid you can't handle this much woman?'

'I'm Rick Jarrett,' he replied. 'Been a long time travelling, all I want's a place to sleep.'

The painted lips turned down. 'Maybe you just ain't much of a man.'

'Maybe, but there's nothing wrong with my eyesight,' Jarrett said, looking at the powder spilling from her face and neck onto the frayed silk.

She dashed half a glass of whiskey into his face. 'You skunk!'

'Always know when I've met a lady,' he wiped his face, lips curling into a grin. 'I think you'll find it's that dog outside causing the stink.' Behind them the solitaire player chuckled.

For a second Jarrett thought the woman might follow through with the empty glass, and he stood balanced on his toes, ready to side-step. Then she shrugged. 'Guess you've got your eyes on the kid, same as the rest of 'em,' she said, glancing at the girl. 'Like your flesh young and tender. Have to wait for the auction. There's gonna be a whole lot of dogs all sniffin' after the same bitch.'

'I'd say she's not much more than a pup,' Jarrett said, 'not ready to be leaving her ma.'

Before Lily Godine could answer the swing doors opened. The first man through looked as if he could be Felipe's brother, except he weighed in twice as heavy. The second was white, though his face was weathered to the colour of the saloon counter. A vivid scar in the shape of a question mark stood out on his right cheek. 'Hi Lily. Got a couple of glasses to go with that bottle? Me an' Ramirez worked up quite a thirst.'

There was a jingle of spurs on the sidewalk and a ginger-haired youth edged in behind the men. Seeing the girl he grinned and veered around the tables towards her.

Lily favoured the newcomers with a smile. 'Sure thing, Hook. Ain't you buyin' Jude a drink?' she asked innocently, looking at the youngster. 'I got a bottle of sarsaparilla under the counter.'

'Hell, I ain't a kid, I done my share of the work, I'll have whiskey.' The youth scowled and grabbed the girl's arm. 'Melia, you better not be laughin' at me. Don't you know you're supposed to say hello real nice when folks come in?'

The girl faced him, a flush of colour rising up her neck to her cheeks. Seeing her clearly for the first time Jarrett felt a surge of some powerful emotion; the child was a beauty, with perfect features in a heart-shaped face that right now was alight with fury. She pulled away from the boy to strike at him with the broom but the handle swung wide and slammed against the legs of the chair where the bald man lay sleeping.

The result was spectacular. The plump figure crashed to the floor, the chair splintering beneath him. The impact as his buttocks hit the boards shook the whole room and a cloud of dust rose to the ceiling.

The girl shrank back against the wall with her eyes on Lily Godine and the broom clutched tight to her chest as if for protection. The shards of the broken bottle lay round her bare feet and there was a bead of blood on one of her toes.

As soon as he had breath enough the bald man began on a few well-chosen words, then he rolled to one side and his eyes fell on the girl's legs. He snapped his mouth shut.

26

Without uttering another sound the plump figure hauled himself upright and left, limping a little, ignoring the laughter that followed him. The girl stood as if turned to stone, staring at the wreckage.

'Don't just stand there, Melia, get that mess cleared up,' Lily commanded, her voice hard. 'And you'd better start bein' more careful girl, Mr Vosper won't thank you for upsettin' his customers.'

Jarrett finished his whiskey and set the glass down in front of the barman. 'Rooms?' He prompted.

'Out back.' The man shifted the pipe into the side of his mouth and jerked his head at a list of charges, browned almost to illegibility by years of smoke. 'Clean sheets is extra.'

A hour later Jarrett lay in a hot bath, running a hand down the smooth soreness of his clean-shaven jaw. Steam rose from the rapidly cooling water; Capelli's barber shop was the only place in town to boast hot baths, but there wasn't much call for them until the spring and there was no fire in the grate.

Jarrett stretched his hand towards the Winchester propped beside the tub as the door creaked open, but it was only a kid of about fifteen carrying a fresh can of hot water and a couple of towels. 'Mr Capelli said you'd want these.' The boy's features twisted around and settled into a vacant open-mouthed smile.

'Thanks.' Jarrett had a sudden idea. 'What's your name?'

'Hoby.'

'You work for Mr Capelli all the time, Hoby?'

The boy frowned, thinking about it. 'Just when he wants something done,' he said at last. 'Work for anybody if they pay me,' he finished brightly.

'Then how would you like to earn a dollar?'

'A whole dollar?' The youngster's eyes widened.

'That's right. And the job won't take you long. There's a dead dog up the street a ways. It needs burying.'

Hoby nodded. 'Yeah, I seen it.'

'Smelt it too, I bet,' Jarrett said. 'I swear that stench is following me. You can't bury the dog right where it is, because the wagon wheels will just dig it up again, savvy? You drag it up the hill first and find a place where the sun's melted the ice.' Jarrett watched the slow working of the boy's mind behind his slack features until light dawned. 'You know somebody who'll lend you a shovel and a rope?'

'Sure. A whole dollar?'

'That's right.' He stretched across and pulled a coin from his pocket. 'Look, there's a quarter you can have now, I'll give you the rest when the job's done, OK?'

The big head nodded violently and the boy left at a clumsy run. Jarrett grinned and took a deep breath of air before sliding his head under the water. When he surfaced again the barber was standing beside the tub, his waxed moustache bristling.

'What you do to the boy?' Capelli asked angrily.

'Gave him some money to do a little job for me,' Jarrett replied. 'Sorry, I didn't think he'd run straight off like that.'

The little Italian gave him a long hard look. 'Guess it don't matter. He's a good boy but he's not too bright.'

'Tell me something Mr Capelli, when did folk start calling this town Vosperville?'

The mouth beneath the moustache drew into a tight line. 'A while ago,' Capelli said, then he turned and left, sending an icy draught round Jarrett's head and shoulders as he slammed the door shut behind him.

Jarrett went back to stroking his smooth chin. A barber who didn't care to talk struck him as unnatural. But then it looked as if there were quite a few things wrong in this neighbourhood.

CHAPTER FOUR

Jarrett sniffed the morning air. The town didn't exactly smell sweet but the absence of the dog's carcass was a great improvement. He brushed crumbs off his vest and let the door of the cantina swing shut behind him, looking along to the wharf then up the main street. On the hill beyond the town a solitary house overlooked the rest, a huge white-painted mansion built on a level shelf where the trees had been cleared. Dominating the front was a fancy stone portico that looked as if it belonged in some large city; here in Harper's Mill it was crazily out of place.

As he turned to walk up the street, passing the saddlers and the funeral parlour on his way to the general store, Jarrett pondered on the mansion on the hill. The stone pillars must have been shipped from hundreds of miles away. What sort of man built a house like that in the middle of a forest?

Outside the store a man in a brown coat stood on the sidewalk with his deeply-lined face angled to catch the warmth of the sun.

'Morning,' Jarrett said, 'Feels like the thaw's coming. You open for business?'

'Guess so.' The storekeeper ran a hand over his thin grey hair. He looked to be about sixty, running a little to fat. Opening the door for his customer he tucked his head down as if he didn't want to meet Jarrett's eyes. 'What was it you wanted?'

After the brightness of the street it was dark inside, but there was enough light to show that the shelves were mostly empty. A half sack of dried maize stood on the floor alongside a jar of salt. The only thing on the counter was a basket of eggs. 'Looks like I could be unlucky,' Jarrett said. 'I was hoping to write a letter. Need a pen and paper and ink.'

'Sure, those I have, just don't ask for flour or coffee. Use of pen and ink's free at the mail or the dispatch office down at the wharf.'

'Prefer to buy my own,' Jarrett said.

'Fine by me.' The man slipped behind the counter and bent down, coming up red-faced a minute later, his hands full. 'How much paper you want?'

Once the transaction was over Jarrett headed for the door.

'You come here to work for Vosper?' The storekeeper asked suddenly.

Jarrett turned back to meet the man's wary expression. 'My horse is lame,' he said. 'Needs a rest. What happened to your stock?'

'This an' that. Delivery got held up last fall. Didn't make it here before the freeze.'

A woman appeared from the back room, drying her hands on her apron. 'Bert, come while it's good and hot . . .' She broke off when she saw Jarrett. 'Sorry, I didn't hear the door.' She looked at him curiously, her faded blue eyes smiling. 'You'll be the one who paid to get rid of that dog. Thought we'd have to wait till the coyotes got brave enough to come into town for it. Mister, I just filled the pot, why don't you come join us for a cup of coffee?'

Snatching off his hat, Jarrett nodded acceptance. 'That's kind, Mrs . . .'

'Henderson. I'm Annie and this is Bert. Saw you come out of José's place. I know for a fact he ran out of fresh beans last week. Whole town's running dry, we're down to our last half pound.'

'Then it's generous of you to share, ma'am. The name's Rick Jarrett.' He shook hands and followed Annie Henderson through into her kitchen. A pot of coffee big enough to serve a dozen steamed on the black stove.

A quarter hour later Jarrett shook his head reluctantly as Annie Henderson offered to fill his cup for the fourth time. 'No thanks, reckon I'm full.'

The bell above the shop door jangled and Bert Henderson got up. Jarrett wondered if he imagined the warning look the storekeeper gave his wife as he went. The old couple had been friendly enough but they'd told him nothing. 'Mrs Henderson, I've asked a few folk but I don't seem able to get an answer. How long has this place been called Vosperville?'

'Vosperville!' She spat the word out like a curse. 'Harper's Mill was a good town until that man came, must be two years since. Now most decent folk can't wait to get out. There's been a dozen families leave already, but Bert and I can't go. We paid for that last lot of stock when we placed the order, just about all we had was tied up in it. Can't even cut our losses and run, seeing we don't have enough money left to buy a team of horses.'

'I'd have thought it was easier to leave by water,' Jarrett said.

She shook her head. 'Durgan Vosper owns the boats. He'd take the store and every last thing in it and give us no more than a trip down river in return, and we're not desperate enough to settle for that, not yet. Trig Rawlings has always treated us fair in the past, he might still get here. Last October Bert paid him to bring up what we

31

needed from the city, figured he'd put it on sledges like they use for the lumber, but it's likely Vosper's men stopped him. Snow's been too deep for wagons up to now.' She sighed. 'Fact is, if Trig don't come soon the trail will turn to mud and he'll never get through.'

'You don't think he ran out on you?'

'I hope not.' She looked suddenly old, her shoulders slumping. 'Maybe it doesn't matter. Vosper's planning to open his own store down by the wharf and any day now the boat will bring in the stock. Nobody in town wants to buy from him, but if it's that or starve . . . You can be sure the prices will be higher than they are here.'

She glanced towards the door, they could just hear her husband's voice as he spoke to a customer. 'I may be getting old but I still know a good man when I see one, Rick Jarrett. I don't mind telling you, this town's in a bad way when we have to watch who we talk to for fear of Vosper and that so-called marshal of his.'

'So-called? Bergquist?'

'They claim he was elected fair and square, but every lumber man in the territory was brought in from the forest and given a vote to make sure it went the way Vosper wanted. The man who stood against Bergquist up and left right after, guess you couldn't blame him. Only law left in this town is Vosper's law.'

She gave a grim smile. 'Till you came nobody dared bury that dog. Vosper shot it because it barked at those fancy horses he drives. Every soul in Harper's Mill was afraid if they moved the body he'd think it belonged to them. Even when he's not here most of Harper's Mill's still running scared.'

'He's out of town?'

'Been gone since February. They say soon as the ice is thin enough to cut through he'll be on the first boat. I hope it goes to the bottom of the river and him with it,' she added vehemently.

Bert Henderson put his head round the door. 'Annie, somebody needs your help.'

Jarrett rose and followed her to the door. 'Thanks again for the coffee. Guess I'll be going. Haven't checked on my horse yet.'

'If you left it with Chalky it'll be fine,' Bert told him. 'Best man with a horse in the whole territory.'

'I didn't see him yesterday, just a kid.' Jarrett said.

There was only one customer in the store. She stood in the shadows by the door, her hands clasped in front of her; it was the young girl from the saloon, still clad in the dull brown dress she'd worn the day before. At the sight of Jarrett she turned her head away as if she was suddenly interested in the solitary jar of peaches gathering dust on the lowest shelf.

'Hello, Melia,' Annie said. 'This is real nice, we don't often see you in here. What can I do for you?'

Jarrett tipped his hat at Annie and the girl but he paused in the doorway, watching the men working on the foundations of the new building.

'Must have been quite a fire,' he commented, nodding at the blackened patch of earth.

Bert Henderson came to stand beside him but said nothing and in the silence Jarrett heard the girl whispering to Annie.

'I thought to get something to wear,' she was saying. 'Hoby gave me the money. I didn't want to take it, but he was getting upset. It's not like he means anything, not like the others . . .'

'Let me see.' Annie inspected the coins the girl had put into her hand. 'Now where on earth did Hoby get that much?'

Jarrett turned to look at the girl and she flushed. 'From him.'

'For burying the dog,' he explained.

Annie did her best to hide her smile. 'Well now, that's real kind of Hoby giving you a present, Melia. What were you hoping to buy?'

'Would that be enough for a dress?' The girl sounded suddenly very young.

'Well . . . I doubt we've got anything to fit you. Suppose I sell you some of this printed cotton? I've got a piece that would suit you real well.'

'I wouldn't know how to fix it up,' the girl replied.

'Anyone can sew. I'll cut out and give you a hand with the stitching. Come on, let's go and get you measured.' Annie put her arm around the girl and led her into the kitchen, giving Jarrett a wink as they retreated.

'Where'd the kid come from?' Jarrett asked as he followed Bert onto the veranda. 'That woman at the saloon talks like she owns her.'

'A bunch of settlers were coming upriver and their boat went down in a storm. Melia and Hoby were the only ones who survived. She's been with Lily over a year now.'

'A saloon's no place for a child.'

Henderson turned away, his face bleak. 'Least she don't go hungry,' he said.

The livery stable seemed to be deserted. Jarrett looked around and located his horse. The animal looked a lot better than when he'd left it the day before but it was still resting its near hind and it pulled away when he tried to pick up the hoof.

'It's just a corn.' The voice came from behind him and Jarrett whirled round; he hadn't heard anyone come in. He found himself facing the short bullet-headed man whom he'd last seen falling so spectacularly to the floor of the saloon. 'Name's Chalky White.'

The bald man offered a chubby hand and a surprisingly

firm grip. 'I took off the shoe and pared down the horn, reckon he'll be sound in a week or so.'

'Thanks. I'm Rick Jarrett.' He glanced round. There were only two other horses in the place, one of them a sway-backed draught mare. 'Doesn't look like you're doing much trade.'

'Quiet time of year,' the man replied.

'You don't supply the loggers with horses?'

Chalky looked at him sharply, a new caution in his eyes. 'Not since Audie Harper died. What's it to you, mister?'

'Just curious,' Jarrett said. 'It doesn't seem there's much to keep folks here, not unless they're working for the lumber company, yet I'd say this was a busy little town not so long ago. Lucky that fire you had didn't spread. How'd that happen?'

The other man turned away to fork some hay for the old mare as if he hadn't heard the question. 'You'll need a short shoe put on that foot when you get your horse shod,' he said. 'I can do it for you if you want, or there's a smithy upriver from the wharf a ways.'

Jarrett's lips twisted. Apart from Annie Henderson it seemed nobody wanted to talk to him. 'Thanks,' he said again, heading for the street.

A bunch of men were coming up the hill, maybe ten or a dozen, milling around as if there was something in their midst that was holding their attention. Snatches of talk and laughter drifted before them and Jarrett paused on the sidewalk to watch. Suddenly a body appeared, hoisted above the rest, a round pale face topping thin shoulders. It was Hoby. The men around him were cheering and good humoured, but the youngster looked terrified.

'C'mon kid, play the hero.' A huge man cuffed the boy round the head and Jarrett recognised Brossman. 'Only man in Vosper brave enough to dig a hole fer the dawg!'

'Perhaps he don't notice the smell!' Felipe scurried

35

alongside his huge friend, his hands as ever hidden beneath the filthy blanket. 'He stink pretty good too.'

'Maybe we should clean him up some,' another man yelled, dashing to the front of the group and brandishing a shovel. 'Let's find him a real nice place to soak in. Least we can do, eh boys?'

'Yeah, snow's meltin', good time for a bath!' They cheered again and Hoby was hoisted to their shoulders. He couldn't keep his balance, his ungainly body flopping down so he was jostled around on his back.

The simpleton twisted and turned, his face contorted by fear. 'I didn't do nothin'!' he yelled, his voice rising to a squeal. His tormentors ignored him and moved on, increasing their pace.

Bergquist stood outside the saloon surveying the scene, his thumbs hitched into his belt. Jarrett stepped across to join him. 'Marshal? Are you going to stand by and watch this?'

The man turned indifferent eyes on him. 'Don't rightly see how I can stop 'em. Besides, it's just a bit of fun.'

'But he's weak in the head, they're scaring him out of what little wit he's got. What sort of lawman are you?'

'A live one, and I plan to stay that way. You sure like interferin' in other folks business, mister,' the marshal said laconically. 'You want to tell 'em to quit then go ahead, I ain't about to stop you.'

CHAPTER FIVE

Jarrett hurried to his room and grabbed the Winchester. Half-wit or no, Hoby had been working for him when he buried the dog's carcass and he couldn't let them torment the kid. Trouble was one man with a rifle wouldn't stand much chance against a dozen, no matter how good he was with a gun; he needed an edge. He felt to check the scrap of metal was still hidden under his belt.

Stepping back through the door Jarrett didn't notice the figure pressed up against the wall in the passage. There was a slight sound behind him and an explosion of light seared through his brain. There was barely time to register that he'd been poleaxed before the floorboards connected hard with the front of his skull and the world turned dark.

Later, how much later he didn't know, Jarrett woke with a sour mouth and a throbbing head, trying to recall how he came to be lying on the floor of a room he didn't recognize. His Winchester lay beside him and he stretched out a hand to draw it close. Squinting against the pain in his temples he checked the rifle was loaded. He groped his way to his knees then onto the side of the bed to sit with the Winchester across his lap, the room revolving around him.

There was the click of a key turning in a lock and the

door opened, making more noise than his head wanted to deal with. He cocked the rifle and straightened up to look at the pale shape in the doorway. It was a young girl with a cloud of dark hair around her face. The sight of her brought a name to mind; he tried to form it into a word but the sound stuck behind his teeth. Then she spoke and the illusion dissolved into the past. This was Melia, the kid from the saloon at Harper's Mill. The flesh around her eyes was red and swollen.

'You feeling better?' she asked.

'Somebody hit me,' he said, exploring the tender spot on the back of his skull with tentative fingers.

She nodded. 'That was me.'

'You?' His anger sent her cowering back to the doorway, but he was in no state to harm her, wincing as the sound of his own voice slice painfully through his head. 'Why?'

'You were going to help Hoby. But that's what they wanted. They'd have killed you.'

'Vosper's men?' Jarrett asked.

The girl nodded. 'Felipe and Ramirez planned to get you away from town. Everyone here belongs to Vosper,' she said. 'Except the ones who're too scared to show their faces when there's trouble. I thought if you didn't turn up they'd let him go.' Her eyes glistened with new tears. 'Guess I was wrong.'

'Why? What happened?' He prompted.

'They came back a while ago, but I can't find Hoby. He's not at Mr Capelli's or the cantina.'

The ice was thawing slowly but there was a raw wind blowing off the river as Jarrett strode up the street towards the trees. Looking back he saw the girl following him. She'd wrapped a thin shawl over her dress but she was shuddering with the cold and her bare feet were blue. He waited for her to catch up and took off his coat, draping it over her shoulders. 'You'd be better staying inside,' he said.

'They might have left a couple of men up here to wait for you.'

He was amused, wondering what she thought she'd do in his defence, and she turned away from his smile. 'I saved your life,' she reminded him angrily.

'Maybe. Or maybe I could have got Hoby out of trouble. Guess you don't have much faith in me.'

'I don't have faith in nobody.'

Tracks in the mud led them up into the trees and across the hillside to where a patch of freshly turned earth showed the dog's last resting place; Hoby had made a good job of it, piling stones on top to keep out the coyotes. They found him in a snow drift a few yards further on, curled up in a ball, long arms hugging his shivering knees, his head resting on a tree stump. The vacuous face was barely recognisable; both eyes were swollen shut and his nose was bloody. Melia threw herself down on her knees to touch the boy's bruised cheek. 'Hoby?'

The youngster took no notice, a faint crooning moan issuing from his lips. Jarrett crouched to lift the boy off the ground but Hoby resisted, the moan rising to a scream.

'Come on, kid, let's get you out of here. I'll need that coat back, Melia.' She'd already shrugged out of it and now she pushed Jarrett aside, gentling Hoby as she might a frightened animal, hushing him, stroking his wet matted hair. Careful as a mother wrapping her baby she coaxed the youngster into Jarrett's coat.

'Where do we take him?' Jarrett asked, lifting the shivering boy who was calm now though still sobbing quietly. 'This place got a doctor?'

'Not since last fall,' Melia said, her teeth chattering in the chill air. 'But Mr Capelli took care of Ged Dwyer when he broke his arm, and Mrs Capelli's real kind.'

'The barber-shop then. You'd better move before you

freeze where you stand. Run on ahead and tell them we're coming.'

Daylight was fading into night and the temperature was falling fast. Hoby was all arms and legs, his weight no burden at all for Jarrett as he hurried back into town. Though the day was almost over there were still folks about but nobody acknowledged him, men turning away as he approached as if he had something contagious. He grimaced. It was Harper's Mill that was sick, and he was beginning to think the town was too far gone to save.

Bergquist stepped out of the shadows as Jarrett rounded the front of the Double Eagle. 'He still alive?' he asked.

'No thanks to you.' Jarrett hurried on, aiming for the light spilling from the door of the barber-shop. Melia stood there waiting with a plump dark-haired woman.

'Things got out of hand,' Bergquist said, following along behind. 'The boys came and told me. It was just a bit of fun, only Hoby started punchin' and kickin' an' would-n't quiet down. They didn't have no plans to leave him out there, seems he ran off.'

'Sure. They must have looked real hard.'

Bergquist shrugged. 'These things happen.'

'Man with a badge might have stopped it happening,' Jarrett said bleakly. 'You've got the badge, but you're not much of a man.' He didn't wait for the marshal's response, leaving him behind and shouldering his way into the warmth of the barber-shop.

Hovering between sleep and waking, Jarrett opened his eyes to see Melia standing in the doorway of his room again. This time she had a steaming bowl in her hands. He loosed his hold on the Winchester and sat up on the bed, cursing his carelessness; he'd left the door unlocked and the lamp burning. Sounds from the saloon suggested the place was full and he guessed it must be past midnight.

'I slipped out and went to see Hoby,' the girl said. 'He's real sick, can't seem to breathe. Mr Capelli thinks he's likely got pneumonia from lying out in the snow. Your head still hurt?'

'It's been better,' Jarrett admitted.

'This might help, there's some herbs in here that are real good for bruises.'

'Bruises? It's a wonder you didn't break my skull. What did you use on me?'

'That.' She nodded at the battered warming pan lying on the floor. 'I'm sorry.'

'Come in and shut the door.' He swung his legs round to sit on the side of the bed. 'If you really want to help, you can answer some questions for me.'

'All right, so long as you let me tend your head.' She put the bowl on the wash stand and squeezed out a rag that was floating in the water. 'Stay still.'

He winced, but her touch was gentle. 'Tell me, Melia, the building across the street that burnt down, what was it?'

'The church. It was real fine, all sort of light and shiny inside. Father Martin held a special service every year for my ma and pa and the other folks who were drowned.'

'Father Martin? I haven't seen him. What happened, did he leave town once the church was gone?'

There was a pause, the only sound the drip of water as she wrung out the rag again. 'He's dead. He died in the fire.'

There was another silence. 'How come?' Jarrett said at last.

'We'd been trying to put the fire out, half the town was lined up with buckets, dragging water out of the river, but it was no good, the flames were shooting right out through the roof. Then Mr Vosper drove up, and he said the marshal had to clear the street before anybody got hurt. Only Father Martin didn't come. He ran back to the church for something and the porch was all alight and it fell on him.'

'Why did he go back? Why wait till it was too late if there was something he wanted to save?'

'I don't know. Folks say things. They say Mr Vosper wanted him dead. Leastwise he wanted the church gone, so he could build his new mill, but he wasn't even there when Father Martin ran into the fire, he'd already gone.'

'Who was there?' Jarrett ducked out from under her hands and turned to look at her. 'Who was standing closest to him?'

'Two of Mr Vosper's men.'

'Which two?'

'The little one with the mean eyes,' she said. 'Felipe. Him and his friend.'

'Brossman,' Jarrett breathed. 'That figures. So nobody knows what it was Father Martin suddenly decided to rescue.'

'Oh yes, he had it in his hand when they dragged him out. It was the gold cross with Jesus on it, the one that used to be on the table with the candlesticks. I saw it after, we all did. Only it got spoiled in the fire.'

'He ran all the way to the altar?'

She shook her head. 'No, just into the porch. Father Martin only had one hand, he couldn't have been carrying the cross before, or we'd have seen it. Don't know how come it was in the porch, or why he went to fetch it. Guess it was for a new church, only now there's no priest so maybe there'll never be one.'

'I wouldn't be surprised,' Jarrett said. 'There doesn't seem to be much room for God in this town.'

The girl was very close to him and there was a pleasant warmth radiating from her body. Despite the grubby dress she smelt sweet and Jarrett swung himself abruptly across to the other side of the bed and stood up.

'My head feels better,' he said. 'Thanks. There's something else I wanted to ask but maybe you won't want to tell me.'

'What?' Melia picked up the bowl, already on her way to the door. 'I should go, Lily'll kill me if she finds me in here. I'm not supposed to go near men, except in the bar, and then only when she's there.'

'I guessed that. What's this auction she and the marshal were talking about?'

The girl flushed bright red and stared at the floor. 'It's for me. Lily says everything's for sale as long as the price is right. There's plenty of men want to buy me. Just for my first time,' she added, lifting her head suddenly to look at him, her eyes bright. 'Then I'll be like the rest of the girls. But she says first time's special, she'll make a whole lot of money, and she'll give me a new dress, a fancy one like Tabitha wears.'

Jarrett bit back a curse, staring at her. 'How old are you?'

She shrugged. 'Around thirteen I guess. I lost count since my ma and pa died.'

'That's when Lily took you in.'

'No. I lived with the Prentices a long time before that, but they left town. I was too scared to get on the boat and go with them. I thought if I did we'd all get drowned like Ma and Pa. There was other folks would have given me a place to sleep but Lily saw me down at the wharf and soon as the Prentices were gone she brought me here.'

'And nobody objected?'

'No.' She gave a little shake of the head. 'Mr Vosper bought the saloon after Joe Greenwood died. Lily works for him and nobody upsets her, not unless they're ready to fight Mr Vosper's men.'

'And is that what you want, Melia, to be like the other girls at the Double Eagle?'

She shrugged again. 'What I want don't make no difference. I'm here and what Lily says goes. That's the way it is.'

'It doesn't have to be. Lily has no right to sell you, there are laws that say she can't do that.'

'You got it wrong, mister,' she said, backing out of the door with the bowl between her hands. 'This is Vosperville. There's no laws like that here.'

CHAPTER SIX

A knock on the head can do strange things to a man's mind. When the girl had gone Jarrett lay on the bed listening to the sounds coming from the saloon. Gradually they faded and the pounding of blood in his temples became the soft thud of horses' hoofs on hard desert sand. Before him a pair of black ears flicked back in misery as his horse followed in the steps of Blade's grey.

The heat was close to unbearable; even with the brim of his battered hat tipped right down the glare from the ground was painful and each breath seared his throat. Sweat trickled between his shoulder blades and dried there, leaving an itch. They'd have stopped for a noon break if there was any shade worth the name, but Simeon kept them moving.

Marty rode in unaccustomed silence by Jarrett's side, his big frame hunched against the heat. Joe and Simeon rode together in front of Blade, Simeon's big bay setting the pace, seemingly tireless.

In the distance a darker smear appeared on the horizon. Slowly the faint blur seen through the heat haze became adobe walls and roofs; they'd hit their target. At last they were riding between tumble-down hovels into the town. It was a sizeable place, built around the only fresh water for thirty miles. Jarrett's mind wasn't on water but cold beer as they finally entered the silent main street. There was no sign of life, it seemed everyone was hiding in the shade to escape the midday heat.

Jarrett had no idea what told Simeon something was wrong; the shout that brought the riders to a halt came only a split second before the crack of the first rifle shot. There was barely time for the sound to register before a barrage of fire erupted around them, half a dozen guns spitting destruction from windows and rooftops.

Simeon died first. As a bullet brought the big bay to its knees he fell sideways from the saddle, blood spurting from wounds in the back of his neck and his shoulder, his body jerking as another slug thudded into his chest. Joe was down too, his hand halfway to the rifle in the saddle holster when a fusillade of bullets hit his body. Blade was turning, his spurs raking back, his mouth open to yell. 'Rick, Marty, move, it's . . .' His words were cut off as the blast from a shotgun almost tore his body in two. A spray of blood splattered onto Jarrett's shirt and for a split second Jarrett hesitated, staring into the blue eyes as they glazed over.

He came back to his senses at the sound of Marty's voice screaming at him. 'You heard him, move!'

Jarrett dragged his horse around, aware that his friend was already heading out of town; a few yards further and none of them would have escaped; single shots came buzzing after them like angry flies, but Simeon's warning had left the last two men outside the deadly crossfire.

A chance bullet struck Marty's horse and it faltered, floundering on for a few slow steps. Cursing, heaving on his reins and leaning back hard, Jarrett forced his own mount to stop, leaning down to reach for his friend's hand as he jumped clear of his dying horse. Marty seemed to hesitate. Jarrett cursed him and heaved at his wrist, dragging him up across the saddle horn before driving the black forward again, leaning low, each second stretching out to an unbearable eternity as he waited for the next shot to find them.

They were out of range but still Jarrett pushed the black horse fast under its double burden, the heat forgotten. He took a side trail between low outcrops of sandstone and glanced back. There was no pursuit; the men who'd laid the trap had expected to finish them all there in the main street. Either they had no horses saddled and waiting or they didn't have the stomach to come after two armed men and tackle them in the open. He let the horse slow, and realised why Marty was silent as he felt the warm sticky wetness seeping down into his boot.

Jarrett almost gagged as he saw the ruin of his friend's right arm. A bullet from a high-powered rifle had entered above the elbow and split the joint wide open, gouging its way down the forearm to leave a trail of splintered bone and mangled flesh before ripping the back of his hand away. Blood was pumping from the wound and Marty was barely conscious. Jarrett pulled his friend higher over the saddle bow and clamped a hand tight above the terrible wound.

Suddenly getting clear of the ambush wasn't enough; they needed help, and there wasn't another town less than a day's ride away. The trail divided, a set of wheel ruts plainly visible turning east and without any better idea in his head Jarrett followed them. It was like a miracle when the run-down homestead appeared shimmering like a mirage in the heat. He urged the failing horse to a last effort and pulled up by the open door.

A cow and a pig shared a pen, shaded by a woven roof. There was no other sign of life but Jarrett's call brought an old man out into the sunlight, squinting in the brightness. Without words he helped ease Marty to the ground, and between them they carried the wounded man into the tiny house.

47

'I'll light a fire,' the old man said, tying a strip of rag high up round the shattered arm. 'You got time to tend your horse.'

Jarrett would never forget the smell of that little adobe house; blood and dust mingling with the scent of drying herbs that hung in bunches by his head, the roof so low he couldn't stand upright. Just as clear in his memory was the sound of the rusty wood saw as it ground its way through bone, each stroke of the blunt edge vibrating all the way to his soul. He tried not to look at Marty's face, not wanting to meet the fever-bright eyes and see the teeth clenched in agony, gouging through the scrap of leather the old man had jammed between them.

His pulse pounding in his temples, Jarrett shifted uneasily on the bed, turning and lifting his head as he tried to leave the dream behind. For a moment he almost fought free; he thought he was in a room at the back of a saloon, the sound of drunken revelry coming through the wall. He tried to hang on to the noise but it drifted out of reach.

Against the glare of the sun the black's ears flicked back in misery. Every breath burnt his throat, and his head was filled with the thud of hoofs as the five horses plodded towards the distant town. Jarrett moaned softly in his sleep.

The buckboard pulled by Chalky White's sway-backed mare moved slowly away from the undertaker's office, followed by a sparse straggle of mourners. As the trail sloped the wheels jolted across the thawing ruts leading to the sawmill and the wooden box containing Hoby's remains bounced. Bert Henderson ran to stop it sliding off the wagon. Mr Capelli came to help, along with the man from the cantina and a couple more whom Jarrett didn't recognize. None of them acknowledged his presence. There were no women, only Melia, who wore a tattered black shawl draped over her brown dress.

Jarrett put a hand up to his vest pocket, hearing the crinkle of paper there as he touched the letter he'd laboured hard over that morning. He'd never known anything so difficult to write; finding a way to send it without discovery wasn't going to be much easier.

Up ahead Melia looked round and noticed him. She turned and came back. Her face was drawn and pale, old far beyond her years, but her eyes were dry.

'I should have let you go after Hoby,' she said. 'Then maybe he'd still be alive.'

'Maybe. I'm sorry if you've changed your mind about saving my neck.' Jarrett shook his head. 'No use either of us feeling guilty, Melia. You did what you thought was best.'

She looked up at him. 'They meant to kill you,' she said. 'I didn't get that wrong.'

'But they might not have succeeded. We'll never know.' Two of the men had climbed into the buckboard to hold the coffin in place as the procession set off again. Jarrett and the girl followed.

'I heard something else last night,' Melia said. 'Most of the men in the saloon seemed to believe it.'

She looked down at her bare feet as she walked. 'They've decided you're probably working for Vosper. It's the kind of thing he'd do, sending somebody to spy on his men while he's away. Bergquist warned them off, he said to leave you alone until their boss gets back, then if they've got it wrong . . .'

'. . . I meet with an accident, or get blamed for some crime and end up with a rope around my neck,' Jarrett finished. 'It figures. And meantime decent folk like the Hendersons think I'm another of Vosper's hired guns.' The buckboard arrived at the white picket fence and the coffin was lifted out. A lanky figure stood watching by the gate. 'What's Bergquist doing here?'

She shrugged. 'Keeping an eye on you?'

'You go on ahead,' Jarrett said. 'I need a word with him.' He caught her questioning look but ignored it, coming to a halt close to the lawman and waiting till the girl had moved away. 'Morning, Marshal. Fine day for a funeral.'

The cemetery was on a patch of cleared land above the sawmill, and the river lay spread before them in patterns of greys and blues, the ice melting fast. Spring would reach the forest soon and the ground was wet where the sun touched it.

'Why are you here, Jarrett?'

'Paying my respects,' Jarrett said. 'How about you?'

'I mean what are you doing in this town,' Bergquist ground out. 'You're no drifter, you didn't ride this way by chance. Where did you meet Durgan Vosper?'

Jarrett smiled. 'So far as I know I haven't had the plea-sure.' He looked at the little group gathering round the graveside. 'I'm looking forward to it.' The smile vanished as if it had never been as he returned his gaze to Bergquist. 'That boy died because you weren't prepared to make yourself unpopular with Vosper's men, Marshal. I doubt if you're welcome here right now. Why don't you leave these folks to mourn in peace?'

Bergquist stared at him, uncertainty and anger flicker-ing in his eyes. Then abruptly he turned and left, his long legs carrying him fast down the slope.

The thaw hadn't reached far into the ground and the two men who'd dug the grave were sweating as they leant on their shovels. Jarrett stayed a little behind the group of townsfolk, taking off his hat as they lowered Hoby into the ground and feeling the warmth of the sun on his head.

For the youngster this winter would never end. A headstone in the shape of a cross stood on the next plot, and Jarrett found himself reading the words carved on it. 'Father Martin Sallis. Died 21 September 1889'. He stared down at this stark epitaph for a long moment until the undertaker's voice recalled him.

'I believe we're ready, if anybody wishes to say a few words?' Plump and pink-cheeked with a mouth that seemed to smile by nature, the undertaker nevertheless managed to look suitably solemn. 'Since we have no minister perhaps you'd step forward, Mr Capelli?'

'No.' The barber stared down at the mud beneath his feet.

Undeterred the undertaker looked at the storekeeper, but Bert Henderson shook his head.

'Then I suppose it's up to me.' The mouth set into a sanctimonious smile as he took a black book from his coat pocket to read out a prayer. When he'd finished he put the book away, folding his hands neatly before him. 'Friends, we're gathered here to lay to rest a simple young man who never did anyone in this town any harm. We only knew him as Hoby, but I'm sure the Lord has his name in mind well enough. Let's pray that he's moved on to a better place.' He signed to the men with the shovels.

'Hold it.' Jarrett stepped closer, looking down at the coffin then up at the semicircle of people who stood around the grave. 'Isn't anyone going to mention how this boy died?' They shifted uncomfortably under his gaze, none of them meeting his eyes.

'Pneumonia's not easily cured,' the undertaker said.

'Hoby didn't die of pneumonia,' Jarrett said. 'He died of fear. He lay out in the snow instead of going back down the hill where he'd be warm and dry because he was scared out of his addled wits. The boy wasn't too bright but he didn't deserve to die that way. You people have a lawman who doesn't uphold the law and you've turned your backs on what's right because you're just as scared as Hoby was. I reckon this town deserves its new name, it seems Harper's Mill took sick and died.' With that he turned away, sparing a last glance for the headstone marked with a cross.

'You didn't help the boy neither,' a voice from behind him said suddenly. 'Leastwise not till it was too late.'

Jarrett paused. 'I know it,' he said, and strode away down the hill.

CHAPTER SEVEN

The smoke in the saloon was thicker than river mist. When Jarrett walked in the figures of men and women were barely visible through the dark haze but it was plain that the place was crowded. The loggers had arrived on a lumber sled some while ago, riding down from the camp as the sun set. They were making the most of their time, vying for the attentions of Lily's girls and packing three deep along the bar.

A man in a brown coat lay sprawled on the floor directly between the bar and the door, snoring loud enough to be heard above the din. Jarrett leaned down to grab his collar and clear the way, only to have a huge hand descend on his shoulder. 'Mister, Pete works for me at the mill, an' he always sleeps right there on that spot. He ain't gonna like it if he wakes up someplace else.'

'Fine,' Jarrett let go and Pete's head thudded back on the floor. 'No skin off my nose.' Pete's friend nodded in approval, sweeping round to pick up one of the girls in his arms and treading heavily on his drunken friend as he carried her over to the bar.

Through the press of bodies Jarrett saw Chalky White seated alone in the same corner as before, steadily working his way through a bottle of whiskey. At the next table half a dozen men were playing poker, an island of quiet among the uproar, but there wasn't much money in the pot; the card sharp had one of Lily's girls on his lap, and when he threw in his hand he rose and followed her towards the stairs. 'Be back in a minute,' he said.

Once he'd gone a couple of men moved in to take his place, and as the chairs were shuffled around Jarrett was surprised to see Bert Henderson among the players. Somehow he hadn't expected to see the old storekeeper in the saloon. Another of the new arrivals was Bergquist, who sat himself down between Henderson and the dealer. The marshal's face was flushed as he yelled across at the scar-faced Hook, who sat opposite. 'What's the ante?'

'Twenty cents.'

'Hell, that ain't worth settin' down for,' Bergquist grated. 'Seems like I'm the ante man. Let's make it five bucks. It's Saturday night, boys, them as ain't got no money can git.'

The dealer pushed back his chair and reached for the pile of coins before him. 'I'm out.'

Bergquist took hold of his wrist in a bony hand. 'You got money, mister, no call to break up the party.'

Reluctantly the man picked up the cards. Jarrett paid for a glass of whiskey and leant his back against the bar. Nobody seemed inclined to talk to him, for which he was grateful, and he kept half an eye on the poker game, waiting for the whiskey to dull the throbbing pain in his head. It looked as if Henderson was having a run of luck but pretty soon the dealer ran out of stake money. Bergquist laughed as the man left the table, making room for the card sharp who returned from upstairs tucking his shirt into his pants.

After that the play grew serious and even Bergquist was silent except for the calls, his thin face growing redder each time he threw in a dud hand, particularly if Hook came out the winner. Jarrett's eyes were smarting from smoke and lack of sleep, but he had no wish to spend another night riding that endless trail in the desert heat with only ghosts for company, so he paid for another shot and stayed where he was. Gradually his attention drifted, the babble of voices and jangling music merging with the throb of his bruised head.

'Hell!' The marshal pushed his chair back so hard it slammed against the wall. The whole room was instantly silent, the group of drunks trying to sing around the pianola breaking up into discord, one of them slipping quietly down to join the somnolent Pete on the floor. In his corner Chalky straightened to look across at the poker players then tilted back again, but he kept his eyes open.

'I'd stake you myself if I had it,' Bergquist said, his gravely voice slurring. 'Come on, grocer man, you gotta have a few more dollars tucked away someplace.'

Jarrett pushed closer to see what was happening. Only Bert Henderson and Hook were left in the game, and although Bergquist had thrown in his hand he was glaring savagely across the table at the scar-faced man. The heap of notes and coins in front of Henderson had almost gone, but the pot in the centre of the table looked to hold several hundred dollars.

'Let's see your money, storekeeper,' Hook said. 'It'll cost you a hundred bucks to stay in.'

'I'll stake the store,' Henderson said. 'And everything in it.'

'No deal. I hear the store's empty,' Hook said, a grin spreading across his face. 'A hundred on the table, now.'

'Hold it!' Bergquist half rose, staggered and sat back down again. 'Man's entitled to raise the money if he can. Anybody here want a fine business opportunity? One hundred bucks buys a prime site on the main street of Vosperville.'

There was a charged silence, then Jarrett, driven by

what motive he hardly knew, stepped forward, pulling his billfold out of his pocket. 'I'll take it,' he said.

A few men cheered while Hook's supporters yelled insults. Jarrett ignored them, looking down at Henderson. The old man stared up at him, then he held out a hand and they shook. 'Done,' he said. Jarrett threw the notes onto the heap in the centre of the table and stepped back.

'Makes no never mind,' Hook said. 'I got me four treys.' He set his cards down, showing the threes of all four suits, along with the queen of clubs. He leant forward to scoop the pot.

'But I have a straight flush.' Henderson's voice shook as he set down the six to the ten of diamonds. 'Best hand I've ever seen in my life.'

Amidst a tide of shouts and jeers Hook pushed to his feet. 'That ain't right,' he shouted, slamming a fist on the table. 'Outsiders can't bet on the game, hell, anyone with a good hand could show it to the crowd an' get a fresh stake.'

'Jarrett never saw the cards,' Bergquist said, and suddenly there was a long-barreled pistol in his hand. 'Best go now, Hook, reckon you need some air to help you cool off.'

'That hand was void,' Hook insisted. 'You and the store-keeper ain't gonna fleece me, Bergquist.' He turned to appeal to the card sharp who'd taken over as dealer and who so far hadn't said a word. 'What you reckon? You ever see a thing like that? It's cheatin', ain't it?'

The man gave a sidelong glance at Bergquist. The gun he held was remarkably steady considering the marshal was too drunk to stand. 'Money's there on the table,' he said. 'No rule says a man can't transact a little business during a hand of poker. There's always another game, mister. Best walk out of here while you can.'

Hook glared across the table and people began to move

56

slowly away from him as his fingers flexed only inches from the butt of his gun. Then his attention was drawn to something across the room. The scarred face twisted in fury. Jarrett hadn't noticed Melia's arrival but suddenly she was there, standing halfway down the stairs.

'That's why you wanted to clean me out, you sonofabitch,' Hook said, looking down at Bergquist again. 'You figure to beat me at the auction. Well you'd better think again, 'cause she's mine.'

'Not unless you got money to put where your mouth is,' Bergquist grated, a drunken grin spreading across his thin features.

Lily Godine was sitting at a table near the bar leaning heavily against a fair-haired logger, her face damp with sweat so the powder ran in trickles down her plump chins, some of it rubbing off on the man's blue and yellow check shirt. Hook strode across to her, swiping aside a girl who tried to drape herself round his arm.

'You ain't told us when this auction's gonna be Lily,' he said. 'Time you fixed a date. An' it better be soon.'

'Sure.' Lily heaved herself upright. 'Can't have you boys fighting. How about a week from tonight? We'll have ourselves a party, and hold the auction at midnight. I'll put my best room aside till daybreak. Only the terms have changed. I've had a real good offer, seems there's a man wants our little Melia all to himself, so that's what you'll be bidding for boys. Sole rights. Hell, if you want you can even marry the little bitch, just so long as you can find yourself a preacher!'

Melia had descended the last few stairs and was trying to hide behind the battered wooden post at the bottom, her face white as every man in the room stared at her, dwelling on his own private fantasy. A low animal growl swelled to a roar and the girl's arms folded tight across her body as if to keep them all at bay, but the gesture only accentuated the undeniable fact that she was growing into a woman.

'No.' Thick-voiced and surly now, the man from the sawmill who'd defended Pete's right to his favourite two yards of floor rose to his feet and lurched towards Lily. 'You been danglin' this little titbit under our noses long enough Lily, you can't hand her over to any one man, no matter what money he got.'

'Hell Zeke, she'd be no good to you, you're too drunk to get up the stairs.' The logger who said this gave the man a shove but Zeke didn't fall. He spun round and grabbed his assailant by the hair, lifting him high while the man squealed and beat at Zeke's head with his fists. That was all the spark that was needed to set the place alight. With the roar of half a hundred voices sounding like a tidal wave rushing through the saloon, the room exploded into action, fists and furniture flying, loggers against mill workers, townsfolk caught between.

Jarrett stepped through the mayhem to take hold of Bert Henderson and pull him to the door, straight-arming his way past a man with a chair in his hands and ducking under a swinging right cross from another.

'You'd better get that money home,' he said as they made it safely out of the swing doors onto the sidewalk, raising his voice to be heard above the bedlam behind them. Some instinct made him turn in time to see Hook emerging from the fray, looming out of the smoke, cuffing aside a man who tried to hold him. The scar was bright white against his livid red face, and his right hand was coming up from his belt as he flung himself towards them, the gleam of metal from the blade in his fist sending the brawling loggers scurrying out of his way. Jarrett caught the still-swinging door and thrust it inwards with all his strength. It checked Hook in mid stride, expelling a whoosh of air from his lungs as he reeled backwards to fall across the recumbent Pete.

'Go,' Jarrett said, giving Henderson a gentle push. The old storekeeper hesitated for a bare second then scurried away. Jarrett flexed his shoulders and went back into the saloon, stooping to take the knife from Hook's hand before the man recovered, then delivering a sharp kick behind the ear that sent him to join Pete's slumbers for a few hours.

Jarrett worked his way along beside the wall, avoiding the fight and aiming for the comparative calm in the corner. Chalky White had barricaded himself behind his table, and he sat watching the brawl while he cradled what was left of his bottle of whiskey. 'What's wrong,' the livery-man asked. 'Don't you enjoy a good Saturday night ruckus?'

'Not my fight,' Jarrett replied.

'You got Bert out of the room pretty quick.'

'Protecting my interests,' Jarrett said. 'Don't want Hook killing him before I take over the store.'

Chalky snorted. 'They say you're working for Vosper. That right?'

'What do you think?'

Before Chalky could reply the red-haired youth they called Jude came reeling out of the mêlée and landed at Jarrett's feet. Jarrett picked him up and threw him back at Zeke, who welcomed him with a bear hug, lifting the youngster off the ground and flinging him into another corner, his head connecting hard with the wall.

'Ouch,' said Chalky cheerfully. Then his expression changed. 'Look there.' Across the heads of some dozen or so men heaving in a tangled mass, gouging, kicking and punching at anything they could reach, Melia could be seen on the stairs. Slowly, as if pulled by some invisible force, the girl was sliding towards the rumpus down below.

CHAPTER EIGHT

Chalky began to push the table out of his way but Jarrett was already halfway across the room, grabbing handfuls of hair and cloth, his muscles bunching as he flung men from him to clear a passage. Among the confusion only Zeke fought back, roaring indignantly and swinging a huge fist at Jarrett's head. He ducked under the blow and moved in close, taking hold of the man's large fleshy ear left-handed and twisting it, keeping his opponent occupied so he didn't notice the right jab on its way to his windpipe. As the punch landed, Jarrett let go and Zeke sank to the floor, retching painfully.

The drunken Bergquist had hold of Melia, his long fingers wrapped around her ankle. His other fist held onto the stair rail and his skinny body was draped on the steps. Jarrett snatched a chair leg from a man's hand and brought the weapon down on Bergquist's outstretched arm. The marshal yelped and looked round in bewilderment, only to encounter a rock hard fist that caught him on the chin and snapped his head back against the wall. At that point he lost interest in the girl, his hand relaxing its hold as he slid down to lie in an untidy heap at the bottom of the stairs.

From somewhere near the counter came Lily's voice, cursing loudly, and a moment later the deafening blast of a shot gun started Jarrett's ears ringing.

'Next one finds a live target,' Lily shouted, 'so unless you boys want to start digging lead out of your rear ends you'd best clear the room real fast.'

'This way,' Melia said, grabbing Jarrett's hand and hauling him up the stairs. Before they reached the screen at the end which hid the rooms where the girls worked she pushed open a narrow door. Following her, Jarrett found himself in a tiny space with bare walls and floor, no bigger than a closet. There was a blanket folded neatly under an open shutter looking down over a side street. 'You can get out that way,' she said.

'Is this where you sleep?'

She nodded. 'Yes. Now get out quick.' She pushed him towards the window. 'Go! We're both in trouble if Lily finds you here. She'll skin me.'

He climbed over the sill, turning to let himself down as far as his arms would reach then dropping to the ground. The girl looked down at him and he grinned. 'You can't keep saving my life this way, Melia, folks will start talking.'

'Let 'em.' She shuddered. 'You got the marshal off me, I'd say we're square.'

Jarrett studied the numbers written on the thick yellowing paper and tried to make sense of them. He knew enough figuring to check he got paid fair, but the book Bert Henderson was showing him made his head hurt worse than Melia's warming pan. 'You could just give me back my hundred bucks,' he said. 'Are you sure you don't want to keep the store?'

'Certain sure,' Henderson replied. 'Me and Annie can't wait to get out of this place. If you don't take on the business it can stand here and rot for all we care. We've money enough and to spare, it'll see us to San Francisco. Our son's there, along with a wife and a couple of grandchildren we've never laid eyes on. I've already bought a pair of horses and Mitch is putting a new axle on my wagon, reckon we'll be gone in a few days.'

'What about that stock you ordered? Annie seems to think it might still come.'

'It's yours. If selling it hurts your conscience you can send us a share of what you take. I'll write our boy's address down for you.' Henderson turned the page. 'See, we were making a fair profit last year. You'd be set up just fine, apart from Vosper trying to cut you out by trading in that warehouse down on the wharf, but most of the towns-folk will buy from you if they can.'

'You mean if Vosper doesn't stop them.'

Henderson looked up at him gravely. 'That's a risk, and I won't deny it, but none of his men went as far as threatening my customers, not yet. Could be that a man like you won't have the same troubles, they might think twice about starting anything. Look Mr Jarrett, you have to let me thank you. It came as quite a surprise you backing me last night.'

Jarrett shrugged. 'I bought myself a roof over my head. I'm not too welcome at the Double Eagle any more. Me and Lily don't hit it off.'

'You really plan to stay? Folks can't help wondering why you came to Harper's Mill, it's not the kind of place a man happens across by accident. There's talk that you're working for Vosper, but it doesn't make sense. You've been crossing his men ever since you got here.'

'Could be I was just born contrary,' Jarrett said, smiling. 'Fact is, Mr Henderson, there comes a time in every man's life when he starts thinking about settling down. Maybe fate had this place of yours in mind for me all along.'

Henderson looked at him sceptically. 'Can't say you look like the settling kind, but if you've got some reason for being here you're probably best keeping it close to your vest. I know us folks have done nothing to earn your trust. I'm getting old, Mr Jarrett, but that's not much of an excuse for being a coward, when a man's lived sixty years he shouldn't be scared to risk the time that's left to him.'

'But what would Annie do if you got yourself killed fighting Vosper's hired guns?' Jarrett clapped a hand on the old man's shoulder. 'What I said at Hoby's funeral wasn't fair. The kid's death wasn't your fault.'

'I don't know.' Henderson sighed. 'Some of us tried to fight when Vosper started taking over the town. He worked for Audie Harper to start with. Then Audie died and suddenly Vosper was running the mill. Things went downhill fast from then on. The grain merchant, Bill Westerman, he didn't like it when Vosper's men threw half his winter delivery off the boat, and he wasn't afraid to fight back. It was Bill who got an election organized and we voted him in as marshal.'

'What happened to him?'

'Nobody knows. He disappeared one night, we never saw hide nor hair of him again. At the time folks figured Vosper ran him out of the territory, but I reckon he was killed. Then there was Joe Greenwood who had the saloon. When Vosper offered to buy him out he refused; he'd worked in some of the toughest towns in the West and he wasn't stepping aside for a man like Vosper.' Henderson looked suddenly more than his sixty years. 'We found him drowned in the river one morning, nobody knew how he'd got there but we could guess. We've lost a lot of good people from this town the last couple of years.'

'Like the priest,' Jarrett said. 'Melia told me about him.'

'She tell you how he died?' Henderson was bitter. 'Folks still don't understand why he went running into the fire that way. Nobody risks upsetting Vosper by talking about it.'

'But somebody has to know what happened.'

'I guess,' Henderson said. 'Heard a rumour that Mitch Crump saw something.'

'Who's he?'

'The undertaker. Tried to get it out of him once but he ain't telling, though I reckon it has to do with the crucifix. Beautiful thing. Father Martin had it in his hand when we dragged his body out of the ashes, but it's a mystery how come.' He shook his head. 'We got no excuse for standing back and never even trying to stop him. By the time a couple of us went to pull him out it was way too late.'

Jarrett was silent, thinking. It would have been a hard death. 'I doubt there was much you could have done.'

'Feel better if I'd tried, though. You're right, it's like a sickness, and this town's taken it real bad. In time you turn your back and look the other way in case you're next on the killer's list. I'm ashamed of myself, but I'm ready to run, and that's an end to it.'

Four days later Vosperville was in festive mood; the ice had retreated and the river was open again. A few boys had set a fire on the bluff known as Lookout Point, and flames were shooting up into the clear morning air to announce that the first boat of the season had been seen rounding the bend down river.

'You determined to leave right now?' Jarrett asked, heaving on the rope securing the load in the Henderson's wagon.

'I don't want to be here when Vosper steps off that boat,' Bert Henderson said. 'We'll be a few miles away before nightfall. Thanks for all your help, son, and good luck. If we see Trig Rawlings we'll do our best to get the new stock sent up to you.'

Jarrett nodded his thanks. 'There's something else you could do for me,' he said, pulling the letter from his pocket. 'Be grateful if you could deliver this, or mail it if you miss passing through Wilberton.'

Henderson took the letter, a faint frown appearing on his face when he saw the name on it. 'Reckon there's some folk might find that strange. Guess I was right thinking you're no ordinary drifter.'

'Just writing to a friend,' Jarrett said.

'Sure.' Without another word Bert tucked the letter away inside his vest. Annie bustled out of the store, her arms full of blankets and bundles. With everything aboard she threw her arms around Jarrett. 'Thanks for your help, Rick. I'll be worrying about you, I wish you'd change your mind about coming with us.'

He smiled. 'Can't do that, who'd mind the store?' He returned her kiss and lifted her up beside Bert. 'You take care of yourselves.'

Jarrett stood watching until the wagon disappeared then he walked around his new home, inspecting the sparse amount of stock then shaking his head over the account books, more amused than annoyed at his incompetence; he'd have to find himself a clerk. He spent half an hour clearing out the stall in the rear yard ready to fetch his horse from Chalky's barn. At last he locked the door and wandered down to the wharf, taking his time and watching the men working on the new mill for a while. From the size of the foundations it looked like some pretty big machinery was going in there.

The boat wasn't yet in sight, but half the town was down by the river. Felipe was squatting on the sidewalk tossing dice with Ramirez, while Brossman sat on the back of a wagon, his huge feet kicking idly. Young Jude stood beside him and Jarrett grinned at the sight of the youth's impressive black eye.

'It's coming!' Everyone turned to watch as a boy who'd been stationed on the boom halfway across the water came leaping across the floating rafts of lumber, yelling and waving his arms. 'I seen it!'

The street and the wharf were crowded with people. It seemed not a man, woman or child remained indoors, and the mill was silent but for the ever present hiss of steam. Jarrett stepped onto the sidewalk outside Capelli's barber shop and looked across the heads of the crowd. Bergquist had joined the two Indians and they were walking out onto the wharf, while Brossman and Zeke now stood side by side, almost a match in height and width.

Jarrett didn't see Melia until she was right beside him and tugging at his sleeve, her face turned up in childlike anguish. 'I couldn't find you,' she gasped. 'I looked all over.'

'What's wrong?'

'Hook,' she said. 'I heard him bragging to Tabby about getting his money back, then a while later he rode out on the south road. I know it was him, he's riding the pinto he won off the marshal playing poker last fall. He's gone after the Hendersons.'

'When?' Jarrett was already moving back up the street.

'I don't know, a while ago, I tried the store and you weren't there so I went back to the Double Eagle, then I started searching out here.' She trotted at his heels as he strode across to the livery stable. 'He was riding real fast.'

'Then I'd better not waste time. Here's the key to the store. Fetch my rifle. You'll find a box of ammunition on the shelf in the kitchen.'

Chalky was swinging the barn doors shut and he didn't look happy when Jarrett appeared. 'I'm on my way down to the wharf,' he said. 'You got business it'll have to wait.'

'Won't keep you long,' Jarrett said. 'I need a horse.'

'Yours still ain't fit.'

'Then I'll hire one. Or buy it if you want.'

'Sold the chestnut to Bert Henderson. All I got left is that old mare.' Chalky nodded at the ancient draught horse.

'She broke to the saddle?' Jarrett was already lifting down the bar to let the mare out of the stall.

'Sure. What's your hurry?'

'Hook's taken off after the Hendersons. Says he's planning to get his money back.'

Chalky stared at him for a second then went to fetch Jarrett's saddle. 'She's got no turn of speed, but you'll travel faster if you go straight up to the ridge and take the old trail. Look out for a big white rock hangin' over the track, pretty soon after you pass it you'll see the new road the wagons take down below. It turns uphill and the trails join to cross Chinchawa Creek. Don't reckon Bert will have got much further than that.'

Melia appeared, red-faced and out of breath, wordlessly handing Jarrett the Winchester and a box of cartridges. He nodded thanks, thrusting the gun into the boot slung from the saddle and scooping some shells into his pocket.

CHAPTER NINE

Chalky's mare was old and bony but she was bred for stamina and once they reached the ridge she held to a steady lope along the high trail, her thick legs and broad feet ungainly yet surprisingly light-footed on the rough going. The thought of Hook ahead of him gave Jarrett's trigger finger an itch and now and then he touched the Winchester's smooth stock.

Occasionally Jarrett glimpsed the lower trail winding through the thick forest, making its slow climb to the older track to skirt the steep ravine cut by the creek. At last a huge white rock loomed out of the trees ahead exactly as Chalky had described it. They were more than an hour out of town and the mare was breathing hard, her neck and sides black with sweat, but she held her pace, her big hoofs striking a louder note where they hit a patch still held by the freeze.

A gunshot split the silence, the unmistakable sound of a rifle. It was followed by a chorus of protesting shrieks and whistles as birds went spiralling into the sky then there was another report that sounded as if it came from the same gun. The slope was too steep to attempt to ride and Jarrett pushed on, cursing the willing mare and scanning for a route down.

A minute later there was a gap in the trees and he could

see. Far below him a rider was stepping off a stocky pinto, its white rump gleaming in the sunlight. The wagon was slewed across the road, the team turned in among the scrub that lined the river bank. The offsider's harness was hooked up on a branch and it was tossing its head, the wagon jolting as the horse attempted to free itself.

Bert Henderson lay face down in the half-frozen mud beside the wagon, his arms and legs outstretched, while Annie was a crumpled heap half on the seat, one arm draped over the brake lever.

Only a madman would have attempted to ride that slope, but rage was boiling through Jarrett's veins and he sent the mare tipping over the edge. She hurtled down, sliding on her haunches, head up, her forelegs scrabbling frantically to keep her footing. Jarrett dragged the Winchester from its holster, leaning hard back, trying not to interfere with the mare as she plunged towards the lower trail. A missed step could kill them both.

The assassin stood bent over Bert Henderson's body. His head jerked up as he heard the mare's frantic approach and for a fleeting moment he stared at Jarrett, his eyes wide, the white scar clear on his cheek. Hook tucked away the money he'd taken from the storekeeper's pocket, grabbing for the pinto's rein and pulling the beast around as he leapt for the saddle.

The Winchester spoke, an impossible shot with the mare skidding and slithering to regain her balance as she reached level ground. Hook was already running, turning the pinto and driving back with spurred heels to gallop on towards the Chinchawa crossing.

Jarrett sent another shot after the fleeing man then threw himself off the mare's back. Bert Henderson hadn't moved. There was a small fringe of red blossoming round the neat hole in the back of his vest, dead centre. Sparing no more than a glance at the retreating rider, now just a speck of black and white as Hook reached the high trail and turned back towards town, Jarrett gently turned the old man over and thumbed the lids down over his sightless eyes.

The team were plunging in panic, the scent of blood adding to their fear as they dragged the wagon further into the scrub. Jarrett pushed his way through to their heads, gentling them, then easing them backwards a step at a time. With the wagon back on the trail and the team hitched to a fallen tree alongside the old mare, he went to look at Annie Henderson. He didn't like to leave the old people's bodies untended, but he wanted to go after their murderer.

Then Annie moaned. There was a growing pool of blood seeping into the wooden boards that formed the wagon bed. The shot had taken the old woman in the shoulder; it was a bad wound but not necessarily fatal. He'd seen men recover from worse, but this was a woman well on in years. There was no question now of hurrying back to Harper's Mill.

A bloody sun hung in the west as Jarrett drove the wagon into town; it had been a slow journey with Annie gradually descending into delirium. He'd wedged her among the furniture and many times he'd stopped as she tossed and turned, sometimes coaxing her to drink a mouthful of water. At last she'd settled into an uneasy slumber but still he'd kept the horses at a quiet walk; Jarrett was bitter about Bert Henderson's death, blaming himself, and he wasn't about to lose the storekeeper's wife.

Vosperville was celebrating; the arrival of the boat meant there was a plentiful supply of spirits for the Double Eagle, and as Jarrett drove past he saw new faces among the girls at the windows of the upstairs rooms, yelling taunts and encouragement to the men in the street below, many of them already the worse for drink. A fight broke out in front of the off-wheeler and Jarrett hauled on the reins, cursing the drunkards. Then somebody noticed his cargo and the argument was forgotten as a crowd gathered. Among them was the kid who helped out at the livery, and Jarrett called him across.

'I'm on my way to Mr Capelli's,' he said. 'Go ask the undertaker to meet me there.'

'Sure thing,' the boy said, staring for a second at Bert Henderson's feet sticking out from under a blanket in the back of the wagon, then dashing away.

Drawing up outside the barber-shop Jarrett took Annie in his arms and lifted her down. Mr Capelli hurried out to meet them, his little dark-haired wife holding the door open, clucking over Annie's injury. 'Go through back, go on through. Don' worry, Annie, we help you now.' She ran around to lead the way, pushing plates and cups from the table, then waving Jarrett back to the door once he'd set his burden down. 'Mr Capelli an' me, we fix.'

The old barber put a hand on Jarrett's arm, leading him through the shop. 'Is that Bert out there?'

'Yes. I sent a kid for the undertaker.'

Mr Capelli shook his head sadly. 'They was so pleased to be getting away from this place. Nobody didn't expect this. We'll take good care of Annie, you done all you can.'

'Not quite,' Jarrett said. There was something more owed to the Hendersons, something that only he could do. Out in the street the crowd had swelled. There were maybe thirty or forty people watching as Mitch Crump supervised the men removing Bert Henderson's body from the wagon. Jarrett recalled what the storekeeper had said, how he thought the undertaker knew something about Father Martin's death. Now wasn't the time, but he needed to have words with Crump.

He spotted Chalky White among the onlookers and

71

pushed a way through to him. 'Be grateful if you'd take care of the horses, Henderson's not going to need them any more. And your mare deserves a good feed.'

The liveryman nodded and took the proffered coin without meeting Jarrett's eyes. 'I'll see to it,' he mumbled.

Hook wasn't among the men milling round the wagon and he wasn't in the Double Eagle either. At the sawmill Zeke came to glower at Jarrett but he made no move to stop him as he satisfied himself that Hook wasn't hiding among the men working there. Back outside he went on down the waterfront. There was a pinto tied to the hitching rail outside the Shipping Office. Close up the animal was unmistakable; there was the oval patch of white across its quarters that had shone so brightly as Jarrett looked down at the slaughter on the Chinchawa trail.

It was quiet here. A handful of men worked sluggishly on the deck of the boat but there was nobody else in sight. A wintry smile flickered across Jarrett's face; that suited him fine. He leant against a heap of lumber, the cut ends of the trees comfortably solid at his back. Along the street the Hendersons' wagon had disappeared from outside the barber's shop and the mob had vanished, most of them heading back into the saloon.

The sun was only a bright rind of gold over the river when the door of the Shipping Office opened and Hook came out. A last gleam of light sneaked under the brim of his hat and caught the curved scar on his cheek in a red glow. He carried a rifle slung over his shoulder and a pair of saddlebags in his hand.

Jarrett pushed himself upright, lifting the Winchester and snugging it into his shoulder. 'I've been waiting for you,' he said conversationally. 'I was wondering how many folk in this town know you're a thieving yellow-bellied murderer.'

He didn't let his fury show, waiting till it was time for the cold hard core of anger to ignite. It was a chancy weapon, akin to dynamite waiting for the fuse to be lit.

Hook jumped like a jackrabbit, dropping the saddle-bags. He recovered swiftly, snatching at his own rifle and bringing it up as he spun to face Jarrett. 'You talkin' to me?' he snarled.

'I don't see anyone else who fits the description. If you've got anything to say before I kill you then make it quick.' Jarrett began to shorten the distance between them, his eye lined along the barrel, the sight wavering as he moved but centred always on the man before him.

'Sure I killed Henderson, but he only got what he asked for. He was a damned crook, he didn't deserve no fair chance.' Hook began to back along the sidewalk, his intention easy to read; any moment now the last light would fade and he'd be invisible, leaving Jarrett outlined against the paler grey of the river.

'And his wife, did she cheat you too?'

'She was in the way.' Hook was still retreating. 'They shouldn't have kept that money. It's mine.' Across at the wharf the noises from the boat dropped into silence, the men on deck frozen in their work as they watched the encounter.

Lengthening his stride Jarrett closed the gap some more. 'You planning to turn and run like you did up by the Chinchawa? Makes no never-mind to me. I don't care to plug a man in the back, but when I'm dealing with a chicken-livered no-account who shoots old women I could force myself to make an exception.'

Darting a look behind him up the deserted street Hook faltered. There were growing sounds of revelry from the Double Eagle but there was nobody in sight apart from the silent sailors. Jarrett took two more strides then stopped, steadying the Winchester. 'No last words?'

Hook's hands were trembling as he took aim. He snatched the shot and his bullet whined away to Jarrett's right. Jarrett took in a steadying breath and squeezed the trigger, but Hook's nerve had failed him and he was turning on his heel, his booted feet loud on the boards as he fled. The bullet missed him by a whisker and thudded into the wall of the chandler's store.

Cursing, Jarrett followed his prey, unheeding as darkness descended like a thick blanket. He couldn't see Hook, but the pounding footfalls led him past the smithy and the haberdashery store and on towards the barbershop. Then they stopped. Jarrett kept moving, staring into the blackness in the hope of making out his target, knowing Hook would find him a lot easier to see, a darker shape against the water. He had to hope the murdering coward was too jittery to draw a bead on him.

Hook's rifle barked again and something plucked at Jarrett's sleeve. He'd seen the flash but it only served to dazzle him and he ran on half-blinded; to stop and give Hook a standing target would be suicide. The gunfire had brought men to the door of the Double Eagle, a dozen of them spilling out, two snatching the lanterns that hung beside the saloon's fancy name board as they came.

With only the memory of that last shot to guide him Jarrett skidded to a halt and went down on one knee to take aim. Another shot blasted above his head and he did his best to sight on the bright flare from the muzzle of Hook's rifle. Suddenly the door of the barber-shop opened and light spilled out, falling full on the man who stood outside, the smoking gun in his hands.

Jarrett applied gentle pressure to the trigger and the Winchester bucked into him; he soaked up the recoil as his hands worked the action, the process as automatic as blinking an eye. With easy precision he put a second bullet into Hook's collapsing body.

There was a long moment of silence then Mr Capelli peered nervously round the open door, holding a lantern at arms length to stare at Jarrett who was on his feet and striding towards him. The barber was trembling violently. 'I do it for Bert. I think he was going to kill you too.'

'He might at that. Thank you, Mr Capelli, that was a brave thing you did.'

The barber leant back against the door, more words evidently beyond him. With a nervous gesture he pointed at the crowd descending on them, a steady stream of men leaving the Double Eagle, several of them carrying lanterns. The huge form of Brossman was at the front, the little Felipe by his side as usual. 'I think you'd best get back inside,' Jarrett said quietly, reloading the Winchester. 'Be a kindness if you'd take the lamp along.'

Mr Capelli hastily withdrew and there was the scrape of metal as he bolted the door behind him. Jarrett moved quietly back into the shadows to the rear of the sidewalk and put the rifle to his shoulder again as a single figure angled away from the mass of bodies. The man was taller than the rest and he held a shotgun in his hands.

'Be obliged if you'd stay where you are, Marshal,' Jarrett said. 'Just while we talk about what happens next.'

CHAPTER TEN

'Looks like you been interferin' again,' Bergquist said, his gaze travelling from Jarrett's face down to Hook's sprawled carcass, a slight smile on his bony features. 'We'll talk.' He broke open the shotgun. 'I warned him you was good with that Winchester.'

'Good enough,' Jarrett said. He had Felipe in his sights. 'Tell your little compadre there's no call to come any closer. Remind him I don't like having guns aimed in my direction.'

'Sure.' Bergquist half turned. 'You heard him, Felipe. That Winchester's got the range on anythin' you're packin'. Man's already killed Hook, could be he's gettin' a taste for it.'

The Indian scowled and muttered something, but he stayed where he was.

'That's fine,' Jarrett said. 'There's no need for any more gunplay, all I did was settle the score for Bert Henderson.' Dimly seen figures were moving into the shadows to his left to outflank him. Jarrett calculated that he might take Felipe and a couple more along, but if he made a single mistake in judging the mood of these men he'd be among those making a one way trip to the cemetery; it only needed a fool with an itchy finger to bring a barrage of fire his way.

A hush fell. Abruptly the mob split, a dark-clad figure appearing between them, his neat clothes in marked contrast to the rough coats of the lumber workers. Slight of build and no more than five foot four inches tall, the newcomer wore no gun belt and his hands were empty, yet he walked with great assurance, his tooled boots and beaded hat band shining in the light from the lanterns. He passed Bergquist, coming to a halt within a pistol shot of Jarrett. A well-manicured hand swept the black hat from his head, revealing freshly shaven cheeks and even features.

'That was quite an entrance,' Jarrett said, keeping Felipe in his sights but sparing a sidelong look at the new arrival.

'You're disturbing the peace.' The man in black sounded more amused than angry, but his eyes were hard flecks of jet in the smooth pale countenance.

'I'm Durgan Vosper. And you must be Jarrett. I was celebrating my arrival back here in Vosperville, Mr Jarrett, I hope you have good reason for breaking up my party.' He studied the man behind the gun, his gaze travelling up from muddy boots to battered Stetson, lingering only for a second on the implacable face. They were around the same age, perhaps a year or two past thirty, yet a gulf as wide as the Mississippi stood between them.

'I was just clearing up some vermin,' Jarrett replied. 'Trouble is, where you find one rat there's often a whole lot more.'

This brought growls of anger from Vosper's men and laughter from the townsfolk gathered on the fringes of the mob. The laughs were quickly stifled; Henderson had been right, the whole town was running scared.

Vosper's lips curved in a smile but the dark eyes were black holes, deep as hell itself. 'I don't think Hook's friends care to be described that way. You're not in the position to damn the man as a killer when you're standing over his dead body with a smoking gun in your hand.'

'Hook shot Bert Henderson in the back. Wouldn't have been a crime to kill him the same way, but I fought him fair.' Jarrett might not be able to see behind him but instinct told him there was movement close by, he could feel it in the prickling hairs on the nape of his neck.

'Henderson? I recall the name but not the man.' Vosper turned to Bergquist. 'Well, Marshal? It seems you haven't filled me in on everything that's been happening while I was away.'

Bergquist shrugged. 'Henderson's the old man who kept the store. Him and Hook fell out over a poker game a few days ago. Hook thought he'd been cheated.'

'And had he?' Vosper didn't sound as if it mattered much either way. 'Surely they should have settled the matter at the time.'

'Everyone thought they had,' Jarrett said. 'The marshal came out on Henderson's side.'

'That's right.' Bergquist ground out the words, sending a dagger-sharp glance at him. 'Only Hook wasn't none too happy. Guess it kinda rubbed at him like a boot that don't fit, losin' out to an old man who wasn't nothin' but a store-keeper. He took off after Henderson and his wife when they left town.'

'And when he caught up with them he murdered Bert and left his wife with a bullet in her back,' Jarrett said.

'We only have your word for that,' Vosper's voice was soft. 'Just as we only have your word for what happened here tonight. Hook worked for me, and I don't like to be inconvenienced, Mr Jarrett. Nor do I like people taking the law into their own hands in my town.' He looked around, sweeping a look at the men behind him. 'Don't you feel a little lonely? One gun against so many.'

There were several men approaching under the cover

of the sidewalk, a stray beam from a lantern reflecting dully off the rifles they carried. Any second now they'd be in range. Jarrett's finger tightened on the trigger. He could see beads of sweat on Felipe's face. 'If I die here I'll be taking a few of your men along,' he said. 'They might want to think about that before they start slinging lead.'

'Don't . . .' Felipe's eyes swivelled nervously to the figures in the shadows. 'Hey boss, you tell 'em to stop, heh?'

'Your call, Vosper,' Jarrett said. 'Like I told you, what happened between me and Hook was a fair fight.'

'It was.' A new voice broke the charged silence and it took all Jarrett's self-control not to turn and look for the man who'd spoken. A frown appeared between Vosper's neat eyebrows.

'Captain Olafsen.'

The newcomer came into Jarrett's line of sight. A grey-haired man, tall and broad-shouldered with the rolling gait of a seaman, he wore an old pea-jacket with tarnished buttons, but there was an air of authority about him. At his back came the half dozen sailors who'd been working on the boat.

The man stopped face to face with Vosper. 'We see it clear, Mr Vosper. This man tells you truly. The one who died fired first. He never deny he shot the woman. We hear it.'

'Then I'm glad you happened to be here, Captain.' Vosper acknowledged his intervention with a gracious nod of his head. He turned, raising his voice. 'Seems we're wasting good drinking time.' There was a murmur from the crowd. 'Let's get back to the party. First round's on me,' he added.

That brought a ragged cheer. Men began to drift back towards the Double Eagle. Bergquist went to take a lantern from Brossman and returned with it, bending over

Hook's body. Still glowering at Jarrett, Felipe backed away until he was out of range, then he turned, flinging a curse over his shoulder. Flexing his aching muscles Jarrett lowered the Winchester.

'Guess this is what it was all about.' Bergquist straightened, a bundle of bills in his hand. 'Few hundred bucks here. Hey, what's this? I never knew Hook could write.' He was staring at a crumpled envelope, squinting to make out the name in the dim light.

'Let me see.' Vosper took it and moved closer to the lamp. 'It's to a woman in Wilberton. Lend me your knife.'

'That belongs to Annie Henderson, same as the money,' Jarrett said. 'I saw Hook take it when he searched Bert's pockets.'

Vosper hesitated, the knife already under the flap of paper. Jarrett kept his expression blank, struggling to keep his pulse from quickening as the man stared at him. Vosper shrugged then gave the letter to Jarrett. 'I think I've seen that name before somewhere.'

'What about the money?' Jarrett asked.

'I counted it,' Bergquist said, handing it to him. 'We'll make it legal. Come to my office tomorrow and you can sign to say you delivered it to the old woman.'

Jarrett took the wad of money. The corners of the bills were damp and stained with red. 'I'll do that. Could be Mrs Henderson will want passage on a boat out of here once she's fit to leave.'

'Might be you'll want to go too,' Vosper suggested, coolly. 'I don't think Felipe likes you, Mr Jarrett. Perhaps it's not wise to ask you to join us right now, but I'd be happy to offer you a drink before you leave town. Captain, there's plenty of rum, fresh from that consignment we brought upriver with us, you and your men are welcome to sample it if you don't care for whiskey.'

'No. The offer is kind, but tonight we work. When all is

done, then we drink. Tomorrow maybe, or the next day.'
Olafsen nodded to Jarrett and withdrew, the sailors following him.

'The *Solveg* is scheduled to sail on Monday,' Vosper said.
'But the *Fortune* will be here soon. When Mrs Henderson
wishes to leave I'll arrange for her ticket to be issued free
of charge, it seems the least I can do. I accept no respon-
sibility for Hook's action, but since I employed him I owe
her that.' He replaced the black hat on his head and gave
a graveyard smile. 'You and I must talk again soon, Mr
Jarrett.'

'Keep that line taut!' Captain Olafsen's roar carried clear
to the Double Eagle. Jarrett smiled to himself as he
stepped out of the saloon into the early sunlight; it hadn't
been easy to rouse anyone, and he'd enjoyed dragging the
surly barkeep from his slumbers. By rights he should have
been opening the store by now, but with so little to sell and
most of the town recovering from Vosper's party the night
before there seemed no harm leaving the shutters closed
for a while.

'Good day!' Olafsen caught sight of Jarrett on the
wharf. 'Come aboard.'

'I brought a gift,' Jarrett said, swaying as the narrow
gangplank bounced under his feet. 'To thank you for your
help last night.' He took the bottle from under his coat.

'We open this now, yes?' The captain accepted the bottle
with a smile. 'You like risk I think, facing Vosper that way.'

'How about you?' Jarrett ducked as Olafsen led him
below to the tiny cabin. 'You could've walked into a whole
lot of trouble. I take it he doesn't own this boat.'

'No. A storm damage the *Fortune*. Two days delay,
maybe more. Vosper want to get the parts for his new mill
upriver, he is not a patient man. Me and my *Solveg* were
ready to sail.'

'Guess that was my good luck,' Jarrett said, accepting the glass Olafsen offered and lifting it in a salute. 'Thanks again.'

'You are welcome. But I have little time today, there is still much to unload, these big pieces of machine, they are awkward to handle. Tomorrow you come back and we drink the rest of the bottle perhaps.'

'Perhaps. But I came to ask a favour of you.' Jarrett took the crumpled letter from his vest pocket. A rusty stain marked one edge. 'I'd be grateful if you'd deliver this for me.'

Olafsen looked at the writing. 'I know this name I think. This is why you come to Vosperville?'

'Part of it,' Jarrett replied.

When he said no more the captain nodded. 'Safe here,' he said, putting the letter into a drawer. 'I deliver this myself when we reach Wilberton. But now you excuse, I have to work.'

'Me too,' Jarrett said. 'I'm learning to be a storekeeper.'

Olafsen roared with laughter. 'I think you try, but I think you do not succeed!'

A couple of hours later Jarrett was inclined to agree with the Captain. He'd sold some eggs and a couple of lengths of ribbon to Mrs Dwyer, along with a candy strap for her youngest. Fortunately she knew how much to pay. Once she'd gone he sat on the porch and watched the townsfolk tidying up after celebrating Vosper's return.

Melia emerged from beside the livery barn and hurried across the street, keeping a wary eye on the Double Eagle as she came and going straight into the store without looking at Jarrett. He stood up and went to the door.

'I called to see Mrs Henderson a while ago,' she said, standing by the bare counter and fingering the last two eggs in the basket. 'Mr Capelli says she's getting better.'

'That's good.' Jarrett stayed in the doorway, looking at

her. 'Was there something you wanted?'

'Yes. I want you to leave town.' She turned to face him. 'You mustn't trust the marshal, he's just a hired gun like the rest. He does what Mr Vosper says. Those two Mexicans are going to kill you and he won't stop them.'

'They're South Americans,' he corrected her. 'And they already tried. I'm still here.'

'I spoke to Mrs Henderson and she agrees with me,' she said, pouting. 'Nobody stands up to Mr Vosper for long and stays alive.'

Jarrett smiled. 'I can't go, I'm running the store.'

'Two eggs won't take long to sell. I heard the marshal telling Lily what happened last night, he always talks real loud when he's drunk, guess everyone in the Double Eagle heard him.' She suppressed a shudder and was silent for a long moment, her eyes looking at something Jarrett couldn't see, though he could tell it wasn't pleasant. 'He'd kill you himself, only he's seen how good you are with your rifle. He says even if Mr Vosper doesn't give the order you'll probably get shot in the back any time now.'

'I appreciate the warning,' Jarrett said. 'If there's nothing you want to buy perhaps you'd better go before Lily misses you.'

'She won't be up for hours yet.' The girl wandered round behind the counter, inspecting the till. 'I'd like to run a store, I reckon it'd be fun.'

'Like you said, there's nothing to sell.' Jarrett spun round, having heard the creak and jingle of harnesses and the rumble of heavy wheels outside. There were three wagons coming down the street, each of them pulled by a team of four mud-spattered horses and all of them piled high. 'Could be that just changed,' he said, as the first rig pulled up outside.

'Mornin'.' A figure that looked more grizzly bear than

man stepped down from the box and began throwing off a layer of furs. 'Sure does warm up when the sun shines. I got a delivery here for Bert Henderson.'

CHAPTER ELEVEN

'I never enjoyed anything so much!' Melia stood back and inspected the row of shelves she'd filled.

'Glad you're happy.' With the last of his furs gone, the grizzly bear had turned into a chunky bearded man who introduced himself as Trig Rawlings. He swung two sacks off his shoulder. 'That's the end of it. Can't say I'm sorry to be done, another week an' the trail's gonna be knee deep in mud and melt water.'

Jarrett added the sacks to the heap of goods stacked between door and counter. 'Coffee's hot,' he said, 'unless you're wanting something stronger.'

'Coffee's fine. Me an' the boys'll get us a drink later, gotta take those horses out to the lumber camp before dark.'

'Why?' Melia asked, reaching up to stack a heap of blankets on the top shelf.

'Because they're always wantin' horses, an' we're goin' back by boat. Them wagons are held together by spit an' swearin', I don't hanker to drive 'em no further. I've set the boys to patchin' 'em up one more time, some fool who don't know better might offer me a few bucks for 'em.'

'The boat doesn't leave till Monday,' Melia said.

'That information could be real helpful to a man who knew what day of the week it was,' Trig told her.

'It's Friday.' A shadow passed across the girl's face as she took coffee to the two drivers sitting on the step outside.

Jarrett watched her go, knowing what she was thinking. Something twisted inside him. The sooner he got out of this town the better, it was beginning to get under his skin; he hadn't come to Harper's Mill to keep a fool of a girl out of a brothel.

'Sure am sorry about Bert Henderson,' Rawlings said, interrupting Jarrett's train of thought. 'When he hired me he told me there was trouble brewing. Not been the same here since this man Vosper took over the town. Was he behind Bert gettin' killed?'

'Not directly, though folks say it's his fault the town doesn't have an honest lawman.'

'Kyle was hopin' to find work here, but he ain't no lawman.' Rawlings sat down on a heap of flour sacks. 'Ain't no lumber man either.'

'Which one's Kyle?' Melia asked, coming back inside.

'The one with the eye that looks round corners,' Rawlings said. 'Claims to be good with that fancy .38 he wears, but I never saw him use it.'

Jarrett grimaced. 'This town could be just the place for him. If he's not fussy Vosper's likely to be looking for a man.'

'To replace the one they called Hook,' Melia said. 'Mr Jarrett killed him last night,' she added, as if it was a commonplace.

'You're one strange storekeeper,' was all Rawlings said, offering his cup for another fill of coffee.

Spurs rang a musical note as footsteps echoed on the sidewalk and paused outside. Jarrett jerked his head at Melia and she disappeared into the stock room. With the girl out of sight Jarrett stepped behind the counter, his hand falling on the Winchester lying beneath the till. He glanced behind him, checking the door out back was barred; if Hook's friends came visiting they'd have to use the front entrance.

A man swaggered in and some of the tension eased out of Jarrett's shoulders. It was Jude, the young redhead, his thumbs hooked into his belt so the right hand was only inches above the tooled butt of his six-gun. The cocky youth looked at the goods scattered around the store, his glance landing on Rawlings for a second before finally lifting to meet Jarrett's eyes. 'Mr Vosper wants you to join him for a drink, Jarrett.'

'And he sent you to fetch me all on your own?' The skin around Jarrett's eyes crinkled. 'Suppose I say no?'

The youngster scowled, his fingers flexing. 'He asked real polite.'

'Then maybe you ought to do the same,' Trig Rawlings said, looking Jude up and down, making a show of studying his black eye. 'He looks like a punk kid an' he smells like a punk kid, but he sure don't talk like one. Better learn yourself some manners, boy, before Mr Jarrett teaches you the hard way.'

'He's got some grown-up friends, it tends to makes him a mite swollen-headed,' Jarrett said, picking up the Winchester. 'Where's Ramirez this morning, Jude?'

'Mr Vosper sent him upriver to the logger's camp, Brossman an' Felipe too,' Jude replied sullenly. 'You coming to the Double Eagle and meet with Mr Vosper?'

Rawlings shook his head in disgust, putting his cup down. 'Reckon you oughta make him say please.'

Jarrett laughed. 'His lesson'll keep. All this work's made me thirsty.' He nodded to Jude. 'Tell your boss I'll be along in a couple of minutes.'

Once Jude had gone Jarrett put his head round the door of the store room. Melia had half the new stock already stacked on the shelves. 'You sure are good at this,' he said. 'How about minding the store for half an hour?'

Her eyes lit up and she smiled, looking like the child she still was. 'You trust me?'

'Sure. Can't make a worse mess of it than I would.'

When Jarrett stepped outside Trig Rawlings stood on the street talking to his drivers. 'We got two days before the boat leaves,' he was saying. 'I'll pay your passage, like I promised.'

'Figure I'll stay a while.' The man who spoke half turned towards Jarrett, the pale orb of his lazy eye passing over him then wandering back to Rawlings. 'You can give me the passage money extra.'

'That wasn't the deal, Kyle, but we'll talk about it once we're rid of the wagons.' Rawlings raised a hand to Jarrett as he passed by. 'See you in the Double Eagle this evening?'

'Sure,' Jarrett said, 'I'll buy you a drink.' He nodded at Kyle and the other man, 'all three of you. Reckon you earned it.'

Durgan Vosper leant against the bar of the Double Eagle, an unopened bottle and two glasses beside him. If he'd stayed with the party all night his face showed no sign of it. He was freshly shaved and a smell of cologne greeted Jarrett as he entered. Apart from the two of them the saloon was empty.

Vosper poured the whiskey, handed a glass to Jarrett and took a sip from his own before he spoke. 'I wasn't sure if Jude would persuade you to come.'

'It wasn't a matter of persuasion,' Jarrett said, rolling the amber liquid round his tongue. It was good whiskey. 'I came because I was curious. Wanted to find out what you had to say.'

Vosper smiled but his dark eyes were cold. 'Already told you some of it. I don't like trouble in my town. You've made yourself a few enemies.'

'That doesn't keep me awake at nights.'

'Perhaps it should. Hook and Ramirez were friends, and Indians have a talent for bearing grudges. The same goes for Felipe, he won't be happy until he sees you planted six foot deep, and where he goes Brossman follows. Of course they know how good you are with that gun. If things come to a showdown they'll kill you, but I might lose more of my men, and skilled help's not easy to come by.'

Jarrett shrugged. 'I've got no quarrel with Ramirez or Brossman. Felipe's kind of different, he's the sort of man makes me ashamed to belong to the human race, but if God lets him go on living I'll just have to grin and bear it. So long as they leave me alone they're safe from me.'

'But how safe are you?' Vosper's voice was soft as he lifted his gaze. Two dark chips of jet bored up into Jarrett's eyes; Vosper's lack of height didn't bother him at all, he didn't see himself as a small man.

'Set yourself against me and you'll end up dead, Jarrett. I have plans for this town. Last year I shipped two million feet of lumber, and once the new mill's up and running I reckon to double that. A couple of years from now Vosperville's going to be the biggest settlement on the river.'

'Are you telling me to leave town?' A slight smile curled one corner of Jarrett's mouth. 'That's a shame. I was beginning to enjoy keeping the store.'

'You and I both know you're no grocer.' Vosper poured more whiskey into Jarrett's glass. 'On the other hand, you have some skill with that Winchester. I see you brought it with you.'

'Just habit,' Jarrett said.

'A bad one perhaps. You're playing with fire. Captain Olafsen won't always be around to come to your assistance.' Vosper sipped at his drink. 'This isn't worth what I paid for it.'

He poured another measure. 'If you want to stay in Vosperville you have to make a choice. You can occupy a little bit of territory all of your own up on the hill, six foot by two, or you can work for me. A man with your talent could be useful.'

'Exactly what are you offering me?' Jarrett drained his glass and set it down, taking a step away from the bar and tipping the Winchester on to his shoulder.

'As Vosperville grows it will need a better lawman than Bergquist,' Vosper said. 'I confess I'm disappointed in him. The people who matter in this town think he's no better than a hired gun.'

'That could be because he administers the law according to Durgan Vosper instead of the United States Constitution.' Jarrett said, ready to walk away.

Vosper merely smiled at the implied insult. 'I'm a businessman, Jarrett, not a gangster. Sometimes people have to be persuaded to see reason, but there are usually legal ways to get what I want.'

Jarrett paused. 'So you'll uphold the law? Are you ready to prove that?'

'What did you have in mind?'

'There's a kid here, a girl by the name of Melia. Lily Godine's planning to sell her to the highest bidder. The chances are your marshal's going to be the one who ends up owning her. That's not right, Vosper. The way I heard it, slavery came to an end a long time ago.'

As Vosper laughed there was genuine amusement in his eyes. 'And I took you for something approaching an honest man. I didn't have you pegged right after all, Jarrett! Admit it, you've got a fancy for her yourself.'

Jarrett shook his head. 'She's too young to be turned into one of Lily's whores.'

'A brat off the streets?' Vosper was dismissive. 'After a year in a cat house she's not likely to be fit for anything else.'

From above their heads came the sound of a door slamming and muted murmurs of complaint. Footsteps stamped loudly on wooden boards and something crashed to the floor. Half a dozen female voices clamoured indignantly then Lily Godine appeared on the landing with a grubby blue wrap pulled round her, the lavish pale curls hidden under a bandanna.

'Melia?' she flung open the door to the girl's tiny room, her face growing a shade darker as she saw it was empty. 'You wait till I catch that little slut!' The door crashed shut, shaking dust from the ceiling.

She noticed the two men and dragged the robe over her sagging breasts before descending the stairs. 'It's a little early in the day for socialising, Durgan,' the woman said, pouring herself a generous measure from Vosper's bottle and giving Jarrett a hostile look.

'Can't say I admire your choice of company.'

'I'm sorry Lily,' Vosper said smoothly, 'I thought Mr Jarrett and I should get better acquainted, and this seemed like a suitable time. We were talking about the auction. Don't tell me the object of the sale is missing.'

'She can't be far away.' Lily had lost interest in her search. She tossed a second drink after the first then dragged out a chair and sat at the nearest table, her elbow in a spill of beer left from the previous night. 'Where would she go? She knows I'll take the skin off her if she jumps the gun. Seems there's not a man in Vosperville isn't getting hot over that little bitch.'

'Mr Jarrett thinks she's too young to be entertaining your customers.'

'Maybe he reckons I should pay for her to go to finishing school?' Lily laughed harshly. 'I've fed her long

enough, it's time she earned her keep. Besides, she'll
maybe find herself a man for life, be a whole lot better
off.'

'What do you mean?' Vosper asked.

'If the price is right the lucky winner can keep her.
Thanks to your man down south I've got me four new girls
and I don't need that whining trollop. There's plenty of
men keen to take the little slut home to keep their beds
warm for 'em. So, Mr Interfering Jarrett, you just have to
make the highest bid tomorrow night and she's yours. You
can turn the bitch into a nun for all I care.' She smiled,
showing yellowing teeth.

'I don't think that's what our worthy marshal has in
mind. Bergquist's got the fever bad, reckon you did him
quite a favour getting rid of Hook. Still, I hear some of the
boys from the camp are getting up a fund to try and freeze
the marshal out, should be quite a contest.'

'I look forward to it,' Vosper said, 'You see, Mr Jarrett,
if I interfere I'll upset so many people. I'm afraid the
auction will have to go ahead.'

'Then we have nothing more to talk about,' Jarrett said,
heading for the door.

'Don't be in such a hurry to turn me down.' Vosper's
smooth words followed him. 'Take time to find your feet
here in Vosperville. I'll keep my boys off your back for a
while.'

Jarrett half turned, one hand on the swing door. 'Do I
have your word on that?'

'Of course,' Vosper said.

'I'm obliged. They're burying Bert Henderson this
afternoon,' Jarrett went on, with apparent irrelevance.

'Is that so?' Vosper drained his glass. 'Perhaps I'll pay
my respects.'

Jarrett pushed out through the door with Lily Godine's
mocking laughter ringing in his ears. A man was coming

the other way. One eye on Jarrett, the other apparently scanning the street, Kyle returned his nodded greeting and went past him into the Double Eagle.

CHAPTER TWELVE

There must have been close to fifty people following the hearse, the low sun sending grotesque shadows in front of them. The two black horses paced slow and solemn, taking Bert Henderson out of Vosperville for the last time. As the funeral turned the corner Durgan Vosper and Marshal Bergquist came from the Double Eagle to put themselves near the head of the procession, along with the rest of the town's dignitaries.

Melia had gone, hurrying back to the saloon when she heard Lily was looking for her. Despite Vosper's assurance Jarrett's back felt broad as a barn door as he closed and locked the store and joined the mourners in the street. He forced himself not to hurry; he'd left the Winchester under the counter, though he felt naked without it.

Jarrett fell into step alongside José Ferraro. He'd taken his meals at the cantina for nearly a week, but on his arrival the man gave a startled shake of the head and ducked away to join Chalky White. Jarrett tried again with Mr Capelli, but the barber wasn't eager for company either, stepping out of the line to avoid him.

After that Jarrett walked alone. At the cemetery he halted outside the gate, leaning his back against a tree and watching the ceremony from a distance. Annie Henderson wasn't well enough to come, but a clutch of tradesmen and their wives followed Vosper and Bergquist to the graveside, and this time it seemed Crump had no trouble persuading people to say a few words about the dead man.

Eventually the sombre crowd of mourners filed back past Jarrett, talking quietly amongst themselves, keeping their eyes averted from the tall figure leaning against the tree by the gate. Bergquist's glance flickered in his direction and Vosper gave him a cool nod of the head, but otherwise it was as if he wasn't there. Jarrett smiled to himself; there were times when being invisible could be useful.

When everyone else had gone Jarrett intercepted the undertaker. 'Mr Crump.' He stepped out into the man's path. 'Be obliged if you could spare me a minute of your time.'

The undertaker's ready smile had gone. He scanned the hillside as if he was the one in danger of getting a bullet in the back. 'I'm busy,' he said.

'Don't worry,' Jarrett said, 'Vosper's bully boys are out of town for a few hours.'

'You think that makes a difference? Simply being seen . . . What was it you wanted?'

'You buried Father Martin.' Jarrett nodded towards the grave.

'Yes, of course.' The man was sweating now, almost dancing from one foot to the other in his eagerness to leave.

'Then maybe you can tell me how he died?'

'What?' Crump looked terrified. 'It was an accident. The church burnt down . . .'

'I already heard the story,' Jarrett said quietly, 'now I want the truth.'

Crump's hands fluttered nervously at his black buttons. 'There's nothing I can tell you.' He darted round Jarrett and almost ran to the waiting hearse.

Jarrett let him go. Crump's reaction told him enough to be going on with; he'd catch up with him another time. The hearse bowled away rapidly down the hill and he followed more slowly, thinking about his next move. Back in town there were plenty of people on the street and it was business as usual, but Jarrett walked straight past the store, ignoring the stares and pointed remarks of a couple of elderly matrons waiting on the step. At the barber-shop he went round to the back door, only to find his way barred by little Mrs Capelli.

'No come in now,' she said firmly. 'This is not so good time.'

'Just ask Annie if she'll see me,' Jarrett insisted, standing his ground, one foot keeping the door open. 'If she says no then I'll leave.'

'Let him in,' Annie Henderson called, her voice surprisingly strong. He found her propped up in a huge bed, looking frail but very much alive.

'Anytime you want me to go then just tell me,' he said, bending to kiss her cheek. 'I came to say how sorry I am. I was every kind of a fool not seeing you and Bert safely on your way.'

'It wasn't your fault. Though there've been times I wished you hadn't come and found me. I'd be with Bert again by now, instead of being stuck back here on my own.' With a wan smile she met his eyes.

'Guess that's a wicked thing to say. God's given me another chance, and I'll do the best I can with it. I only hope helping me doesn't get you into trouble.' Annie Henderson lowered her voice. 'Bert told me about that letter you gave him, and we decided you came to Harper's Mill because of Father Martin. Is that right?'

Jarrett met her look. 'Be obliged if you don't spread your thoughts around. Is there anything you know, anything you've heard that could help me find out exactly what happened the day the priest died?'

She shook her head. 'Everyone thinks those men of Vosper's had something to do with the fire. Bert says they somehow made Father Martin run back into the church that way, but he doesn't see how . . .' Her face crumpled. 'I mean he didn't . . . I can't get used to the idea that he's gone.'

'I'm sorry, I shouldn't have bothered you.' Jarrett pulled the wad of money from his pocket. 'You've still got your son and his family. This is yours, there's more than enough to see you to San Francisco.'

'I don't want it. Blood money. It got Bert killed and nothing's worth that. If that man had asked we'd have given it to him . . .' Tears ran down her cheeks and he put a careful arm round her. After a while she dried her face and pulled away. 'Crying does nobody any good. I hear Trig Rawlings turned up. Bert would have been glad, he didn't like to think he'd got a man wrong. And you've got a shop full of stock.'

'More than I can handle,' Jarrett said. 'If you want the place back once you're on your feet then it's all yours.' There were dark marks under her eyes and the lines on her face had deepened since he arrived. He put the money on the table by the bed. 'Right now you need more rest. I'll call again in a day or two.'

'Take care of yourself, Rick,' she said, closing her eyes as he walked away. 'Stay out of trouble.'

He obeyed her for just over three hours, which was the length of time it took him to get the door closed on the last of his customers; business was brisk now he had stock to sell. Jarrett's head ached with the figuring he'd had to do; scraps of paper with additions on them littered the counter. There was a lot of money in the till and he stood looking at it for a while. The bills and coins didn't feel as if they belonged to him and finally he closed the drawer and left them there, putting off the need to think about it until the morning. He remembered he'd promised Trig Rawlings and his drivers a drink.

Picking up the Winchester he blew out the lamp, then he froze halfway to the door as a sound from outside reached him. The crack of a rifle shot was followed by a rapid burst of pistol fire, not close but somewhere within the town. Very quietly Jarrett eased the door open. There was more gunfire but this time he could hear other sounds too. Men were laughing and shouting. After a pause there were a couple more rifle shots and he realized what was going on; it was a wonder there was anything left of the old signpost the way they used it for target practice.

Jarrett stepped outside, turning to lock the door. The briefest lull in the ruckus down on the wharf road saved his life. Somebody drew in a sharp breath, somebody who was standing not three yards away from him where the sidewalk ended. Even as the sound registered Jarrett smelt a pungent mix of stale sweat and breath tainted by years of bad food and chewing tobacco, wafted to him on the evening breeze that blew off the river.

There was no time to think. Jarrett was already flinging himself down, cursing his stupidity in not giving his eyes time to adjust to the darkness before he walked out of the door. If he got himself shot it would be no more than he deserved for acting like a grass-green tenderfoot.

A slug whistled over his head as his hands and knees connected with the boards, and he rolled towards the edge of the sidewalk. His shoulder made contact with an upright post and the Winchester flew from him as if plucked by an invisible hand. A second bullet missed him, ploughing a noisy furrow in wood. Something slashed the back of his wrist before he fell into the road.

His attacker could see, but for one second Jarrett

guessed he was out of sight. On all fours he propelled himself into the only available cover, flattening to fit underneath the sidewalk then holding himself still, every muscle poised to get him moving again as soon as he determined what the man standing above him was going to do. For a breathless moment there was no sound but the gunfire and laughter from the riverside. The shooting contest was hotting up again.

The man moved, shuffling his feet, a little this way, then that; he was relying on his eyesight, hoping to spot some movement beneath him by peering down through the cracks between the warped planks. Once, the deafening crash of a shot suggested he thought he'd seen something, but Jarrett's coat was dark and he kept his head down and his hands hidden and the slug slapped into the ground a couple of yards away. The footsteps became more hurried, a frantic dance towards the other end of the veranda. Jarrett smiled to himself in the darkness; the man wasn't too bright, giving away his position like that.

Very slowly Jarrett eased towards the place where his assailant had lain in wait. A minute later he lifted his head over the edge of the wooden boards, in the corner right up against the wall where the shadow was deepest. He had his night sight now, and he could see the dark shape bent almost double, its back to him, questing grotesquely as if it sought to smell him out through the gaps in the boards. The man was too big for Felipe and too small for Brossman, which meant it had to be Ramirez trying to kill him; the only other possibility was Bergquist, but he doubted the marshal had the nerve. Besides, this man was solid and chunky rather than thin.

One slow inch at a time Jarrett pulled himself out of the restricting space, half hidden by the wall, until at last he could get his feet on the ground, then he jack-knifed into the would-be assassin's legs and sent him crashing on to the sidewalk. The man grunted as he hit the floor but he didn't stay down and while Jarrett was trying to get a grip on him the pistol barked again. The slug whined away into the distance and the hammer clicked back for another attempt. Somehow getting a foot beneath him Jarrett barrelled forward and this time he made a better job of it. The two men sprawled together and the gun skittered across wood then thudded onto the dirt beyond the veranda. Now they were equal.

Jarrett clawed at his opponent, trying to squirm up the heaving back with the man twisting and bucking beneath him like a mean-tempered mustang. They collided with the solid log wall and Jarrett swallowed a yelp as pain exploded down his right arm from elbow to wrist, leaving it numb. Beneath him his attacker somehow swivelled round on to his back. Desperate not to let his enemy know he was hurt Jarrett got a foot to the ground and launched himself forward to drive the man's head down to connect with the sidewalk, the impact making an audible crack as his skull hit the wood.

Still not sure who he was fighting Jarrett flung his left hand out with his fingers stiff as they sought a vulnerable spot, eyes or nose or throat. There was only the man's shirt, the thick cloth of a collar stiff with dirt, then he was clutching a handful of hair, matted and greasy. Jarrett couldn't see his assailant's face, but the man was strong. The body struggling under his was a solid knot of muscle.

A meaty fist landed a hefty blow on the side of Jarrett's head and without thought he twisted his hand further into the hair and pulled. Something about the response threw him. He had hold of a beard, yet like most Indians Ramirez was clean shaven.

With the suddenness of a shutter thrown back from a window the moon broke out from behind a cloud. Jarrett stared at the man beneath him. One malevolent eye glared back at him, while the other was apparently admiring the shining crescent hanging over the livery stable.

It was Kyle who'd attacked him! There wasn't time to wonder why. A wave of shock ran through Jarrett as he saw what else the light had revealed; death was only a breath away. Silver moonlight glanced off the blade in Kyle's right hand, coming from its hiding place behind the man's back to slice up at Jarrett's armpit.

CHAPTER THIRTEEN

The chance to live was slipping away, measured in precious slivers of time as the blade drove at Jarrett's body. With every ounce of his strength he jerked his arm down, his fingers still tangled in Kyle's beard. He half expected to pull the hair loose from the roots but the man's mouth opened in an anguished screech and his head came thudding into Jarrett's skull.

Kyle's blow went wide. The knife skimmed across Jarrett's back, the blade ripping cloth but barely touching his skin. Extricating his fingers from the clinging hair Jarrett grabbed his assailant's wrist, wrestling to keep the knife away from his body. Kyle grunted and squirmed beneath him as he strained to free himself.

Jarrett had no feeling in his right hand after its encounter with the wall, so he heaved himself up and brought his knee down on Kyle's throat instead, ignoring the fist pounding at his face and chest, soaking up the blows and gradually increasing the pressure, letting his weight sink into the man's gullet.

Breath hissing painfully from between clenched teeth, Kyle struggled ever more desperately to pull his knife hand free, but Jarrett's fingers ground into his flesh, crushing bone and sinew. At last the blade dropped to the ground.

Kyle was dying, running out of air. Suddenly with one fight behind him Jarrett faced another. Victory was a salt taste in his mouth and a singing in his head. A frenzy as old as time held him; he was possessed by an overwhelming desire to kill his enemy.

With a long drawn sigh Jarrett eased off the pressure and reached for the knife. He needed this man alive. Climbing wearily to his feet he took hold of Kyle's collar. Dragging him from the end of the sidewalk he thrust him into the store. Once they were inside he dropped his burden and lit the lamp. Kyle lay still, his face pale above the bruising on his neck. Crouching down Jarrett touched the tip of the knife gently against the man's windpipe.

'It's time to talk,' he said.

Perhaps it was terror that brought the two eyes into focus together, staring up at Jarrett. The mouth opened but only a faint gurgle emerged.

'Why did you try to kill me?' Jarrett asked, his voice dangerously quiet.

'He said . . .' Kyle's voice was hoarse, ragged with pain. 'Two hundred dollars . . . And maybe a job . . .'

Jarrett had believed Vosper's overweening pride would make him keep his promise to keep his boys off Jarrett's back. Perhaps he thought recruiting a new assassin didn't count. 'Go on,' he said.

'I heard Vosper talkin' to you in the saloon, an' I knew he was a man short. I went in and asked if he was hirin' but the sonofabitch turned me down. Reckoned it had to be worth somethin' though, him makin' plans to get rid of the marshal.' Now the words had started they flooded from him fast.

'Soon as I'd had me a couple of beers I went across to the marshal's office an' told him how Vosper was figurin' to give you his badge when he was done with it.' Kyle swallowed painfully as the blade pricked his throat. 'The

103

marshal was fit to walk right out an' put a bullet in you hisself, only he said it'd look bad, him bein' a lawman an' all. Said Vosper didn't know when he was well off, but once you was dead he'd be real grateful. I ain't no fool. Fact is the marshal's scared of that Winchester you carry. That's why when he offered me a hundred bucks to get rid of you I figured it was worth double.'

'So the money was coming from Vosper.'

Kyle began to shake his head, but the knife kept him still. 'No. That was the marshal. I told him I wanted money in my hand, not some promise he might not be around to keep. He didn't like it but he paid up. Got the money in my pocket right now, ain't spent a cent of it, an' it's yours, mister, I swear, you can take it an' welcome. No hard feelin's. What I done wasn't nothin' personal.'

'Murder tends to be personal.' Jarrett twisted the blade a whisker, watching as a bead of blood, black in the lamplight, seeped into the man's beard. 'Particularly to the man who ends up dead.'

'But you ain't,' Kyle said eagerly. 'I'll tell you the whole thing. The marshal told me to put a bullet in you an' take you downstream a ways while he and them boys made a ruckus down by the river. Didn't think you'd hear me with all that shootin' goin' on. You must have ears like a wildcat. That slug would've got you for sure if you hadn't ducked.'

'So I was supposed to disappear?'

'Sure. Town's so scared of Vosper and them gunslingers of his, nobody wouldn't say a word. Listen Mr Jarrett, why don't you let me go. I'll get outa town. You won't never see me again.'

'I'm thinking about that,' Jarrett said. Unbuckling Kyle's belt he pulled the man's pants down around his knees. 'In case you're considering going someplace,' he explained, dragging Kyle's unresisting arms behind his back and using the belt to fasten his wrists together before ordering him to his feet. 'Come on,' he said.

'Where?' Kyle hung back, his lazy eye rolling wildly. 'Mister, you gotta let me go. I swear I'll clear out of town. You ain't gonna . . .' He fell silent at the look on his captor's face, his throat working convulsively. Jarrett smiled.

An hour later Jarrett walked into the Double Eagle. Trig Rawlings greeted him, then turned to the driver who slouched against the bar at his side.

'See, I told you he'd be here.'

The man nodded, looking at the door. 'Still can't figure what's keepin' Kyle.'

'We'll save him a couple.' Rawlings slapped Jarrett on the back. 'That's good timing, we're about ready for the second bottle.'

Jarrett tossed a coin onto the bar. 'You heard the man,' he said, meeting the lugubrious barman's stare. 'Need a fresh bottle and another glass.' He toasted Rawlings, left handed. He'd washed the cut where the splinter of wood had slashed his wrist but a trickle of blood was running down the back of his hand again. Rawlings looked at him curiously, screwing up his eyes in the murky light.

'Looks like you've been havin' an interestin' evenin',' he said, his eyes travelling from the trickle of blood to the bruises blossoming on Jarrett's face.

'Met an old friend,' Jarrett said easily, turning his back to lean on the bar and scan the room. Chalky White was in his usual spot, already asleep. The poker table was surrounded by newcomers off the boat and the card sharp looked happy, while Felipe and Ramirez sat close by, silent over their drinks. Felipe had discarded the filthy poncho, and he wasn't wearing his bandoleer.

There was no sign of Bergquist and since the redheaded Tabitha was draped around the neck of a sailor it seemed the marshal wasn't upstairs, unless he had a new favourite. As if summoned by Jarrett's thought a tall skinny figure pushed through the swing doors, flanked by Jude and the gigantic Brossman. The three of them walked across to the bar, and in one smooth easy motion Brossman pulled a six-gun from his holster and thrust the muzzle into Jarrett's ribs.

'You're under arrest,' Bergquist said, the shotgun he held in his hands also lifting to cover Jarrett. 'Jude, take his gun.'

'What am I supposed to have done?' Jarrett asked, making no protest as Jude removed his Colt from its holster, taking a pull at his drink and looking Bergquist straight in the eyes.

An unpleasant smile spread across the bony features. 'You killed a man, an' you ain't wrigglin' out of it like you did with Hook. It was cold-blooded murder, Jarrett. Justice comes swift and hard around these parts. You know that, you seen some of it yourself the day you arrived. Don't need to use no tree here in town, got enough wood to build you a real fancy gallows. Sure am looking forward to watchin' you kick.'

'And who am I supposed to have killed?'

Trig Rawlings hadn't moved, keeping his place at Jarrett's side. The rest of the men at the bar were beginning to drift uneasily away from them.

'Man who drove in with those supplies of yours.' Bergquist shook his head in mock sorrow. 'Sure wish I'd listened to him. He came to my office and told me he knew you. Said you'd killed a friend of his in Alabama four years ago, and he figured you'd try to get rid of him, seeing as he was the only witness to the murder. I told him there was nothing I could do, advised him to keep out of your way. Guess he didn't.'

Jarrett glanced at Rawlings, glad to see he didn't seem inclined to desert him.

'I've never been to Alabama,' Jarrett said mildly. 'So I don't see how I could have killed a man there. Let's get this straight, Marshal, I don't figure to get myself hanged because you made a little miscalculation. You're arresting me for murdering one of the men who came in driving Rawlings' wagons this morning. Has to be the leery eyed smelly hombre, since the other one's standing right there by the bar.'

'Quit playing games, Jarrett,' Bergquist ground out. 'You were seen fighting outside your store. You can't deny it, your hand wasn't cut like that when you went to Henderson's funeral this afternoon, guess it was a close contest, but you won. You killed Kyle and dragged him inside. Then half an hour ago you dumped his body in the river.'

'That's an interesting story,' Jarrett said, swallowing the last dregs of his whiskey. Bergquist was a coward but he was a clever one. He'd had this figured out when he sent Kyle to the store; if the murder attempt failed and Kyle was the one who ended up dead the marshal could still be rid of Jarrett and prove himself an honest lawman at the same time. It was neat. 'It's true I talked to Kyle and things got a little heated, but I didn't kill him.'

'I told you, I got witnesses.'

'But you don't have a body.' Jarrett half turned to put down the empty glass, ignoring the muzzle of Brossman's forty five drilling into his side.

'I don't need one. A couple of the boys saw you throw what was left of Kyle into the river, that's enough for me. You coming quietly or do we shoot you where you stand?'

'There's not much law in this town,' Jarrett said, 'but I don't believe you can hang me for murdering a man who's still alive.' He nodded at the group who'd just pushed through the doors. 'There can't be two pig ugly men like that in one state, not unless Kyle's got a twin.'

Captain Olafsen stood aside to reveal Kyle standing between two sailors, his face taut with hatred, his roving eye tilted up at the ceiling. Bergquist stared at the apparition in amazement, then he turned back to Jarrett, his face ablaze with fury. His hands tightened convulsively on the shotgun he held. For a couple of long slow seconds Jarrett thought he was going to get a bellyful of lead shot. Slowly the fire died from the marshal's eyes and he lowered the gun. 'Seems there's been a mistake.'

'Perhaps I should have waited till morning to throw that sack of rotten grain into the river,' Jarrett conceded. 'Maybe it looked bad doing it in the dark when folks couldn't see what it was.'

There was uneasy laughter at that and Bergquist glared around the room. The voices were silenced but quite a few of the men were grinning widely, Trig Rawlings and Chalky White among them.

'Me and Kyle were planning to have a drink together, just to show there's no hard feelings,' Jarrett said, 'then he's riding out of town. Seems he's in such a hurry to leave he bought back one of those horses Rawlings sold this afternoon.' The two seamen thrust Kyle up to the bar so he landed next to Jarrett. 'You got something to say, Kyle? How about that drink?'

The man obediently fished in his pocket, pulling out a roll of bills. 'On me.' He mumbled.

Men crowded around, a babble of talk and laughter filling the saloon. Under cover of the noise Jarrett leant close to Bergquist. 'I don't want your job, Marshal,' he said quietly, 'Reckon it would make me sick to my stomach. And there's something else you ought to know. I'm a God-fearing man, but there's a limit to how many times I'm willing to turn the other cheek.'

108

Bergquist met his eyes for a second, then abruptly he turned to go.

'Leaving so soon, Marshal?' Vosper was coming down the stairs. 'Mr Jarrett will think you don't care for his company.' He smiled as the lawman slammed his way out through the doors.

'Can't deny your courage,' Vosper remarked, pouring himself a drink and lifting the glass in Jarrett's direction by way of a salute, 'But your intelligence may be in question. You'll need to watch your back.'

'The man's yellow,' Jarrett said, 'Even when he was spitting mad at me he didn't have the courage to pull the trigger.'

'Not personally perhaps, but there are others who'd do the job for him. Life comes cheap in these parts, Mr Jarrett. I'd say it's none too wise to make a man like Bergquist into an enemy.'

Jarrett shrugged, not bothering to remind Vosper who'd caused his quarrel with the marshal. 'I surely couldn't fancy making him my friend,' he said.

CHAPTER FOURTEEN

'I never worked so hard in my whole darn life,' Jarrett complained, slamming the door hard enough to make it rattle. The lamps had been lit for over an hour but he'd only just shown the last customer out.

'Always busy Saturdays,' Ged Dwyer said, 'but with Mr Vosper's boat arrivin' this afternoon the town sure is buzzin'.'

'My brain hurts from all that figuring.' Opening the till Jarrett took out some coins and tossed them to the boy. Ged caught them and looked back at him, grinning widely.

'Thanks, Mr Jarrett. But that's more'n you said.'

'You earned it. I'd better get myself a proper shop clerk before . . .'

A sharp knock at the door interrupted him.

'I'll get it,' the boy said.

'No, wait . . .'

'Mr Jarrett?' A woman's voice cut into the silence. 'You in there?'

'Mrs Capelli.' Jarrett opened the door and let her in. 'We're closed. You've been in here three times today already.'

'I don't want to buy no more. Annie send me.' The little woman smiled. 'You look like you had a hard day. You

110

come now and I give you supper.'

'I haven't counted the money yet.'

'You leave it late. No good for the bank now, but Mr Capelli got a safe,' she said. 'If you want we take care of it for you.'

'You've got a safe?' Jarrett was bemused.

'A real good one,' she said proudly. 'It belong to Mr Vosper. They say he don't like banks. He buy a fancy new safe for his fancy new house and he sell the old one to Mr Capelli. You come now and we eat, then Mr Capelli and me help you with the counting.'

Jarrett grinned. 'That's the best offer I've had all day.'

He shovelled the money into a flour sack and sent Ged to see Mrs Capelli home. A few minutes later he locked the door and followed.

Outside the Double Eagle a gang of loggers were climbing down from a wagon, ready for their Saturday night shindig, though by the look of it the saloon was already bursting at the seams. There would be a crowd for Lily's auction. Tonight Melia would grow up fast, willing or no. Jarrett frowned. The girl was none of his concern. He had enough to do keeping himself alive until his business in Vosperville was finished.

José Ferraro was bowing low to a young woman who was leaving his cantina and as she nodded her thanks the lantern that hung by the door caught her profile. Pausing in the shadows by the Chinese laundry Jarrett sucked in a quick breath, staring at the woman and hoping he was imagining things. Kate. Vosperville was the last place on earth he wanted her to be.

He watched her walk briskly away. Even the way she moved was familiar. She was plainly dressed, but she was still a sight to attract the attention of every man who saw her, and heads turned in appreciation as she passed. It looked as if life was about to become a lot more compli-

111

cated. And maybe a whole lot shorter.

While he hesitated the neat figure had turned the corner, going south beyond the old mill where a street of old two-storey houses faced onto the river. Jarrett lengthened his stride, reaching the river front in time to see the young woman enter the third house. He reached the porch only a moment after the door had closed. A glance at the crooked sign told him he was outside Miss Jordan's Rooming House for Ladies. For one crazy moment he thought of knocking on the door, then he turned on his heel. For the moment there was nothing to do but take up Mrs Capelli's offer of supper.

A few hours later the crowd at the Double Eagle had swelled until men were spilling out into the street. Jarrett fought his way in through the swing doors and made his way to the bar, where the lugubrious barman and three of Lily's girls were trying to keep up with the demands of a couple of hundred thirsty men. Finding himself ignored Jarrett grabbed the barkeep by the arm. 'Whiskey. Leave the bottle.'

The man obeyed, scooping Jarrett's money off the counter before he pulled away. Most of the tables and chairs had been piled up against the walls to make more space, leaving only the poker school seated. Bergquist was amongst the men watching the play. The marshal was swaying a little now and then, his flushed face suggesting he'd been hitting the bottle for quite a while.

'Time this town got itself another saloon,' Trig Rawlings said, elbowing his way to Jarrett's side.

'I heard there were three before Vosper arrived,' Jarrett replied, having to shout to make himself heard. He reached over the bar for another glass and poured Rawlings a drink. 'He couldn't bear to share the trade.'

'That figures.' Before Rawlings could go on the sound of a shot echoed around the crowded room.

Lily Godine stood on the landing with Durgan Vosper by her side. She laughed down at her audience, gesturing with the pistol she held. 'Only a blank, boys, just to get your attention.' She waved an arm towards the screen door. 'Come on, ladies.'

There was an almighty cheer as Lily's girls emerged. They'd made a special effort, curling their hair and piling it high, with feathers and shiny beads as decoration. Their cheeks were freshly rouged and lips painted with care, and they wore low-cut gowns to show lots of shoulder and leg and plenty more. Gradually the landing filled up, with red-haired Tabitha the last to take her place alongside the others. Lily raised a hand for silence. 'Just to show you nobody has to be disappointed if they don't win our special prize tonight,' she said. 'Look what you boys have got to look forward to.'

There were a few catcalls and jeers among the shouts of approval.

'Quit the jabberin' an' get down to business!' A chunky lumber man with pale yellow hair tipped one of the poker players out of his seat, hoisting himself onto the chair so he could see. When the man tried to protest he was picked up and tossed into the street.

'Come on, Lily,' yelled another, 'Can't you see the marshal's tongue hangin' out?'

'Sure it's only his tongue?' Lily Godine laughed. 'All right. Guess I can't keep my little treasure any longer.'

A slight figure stepped into the light. Melia had been transformed. But for the look in her eyes she could have been eighteen, a whore like the rest of them, only more beautiful than any. Frills around her shoulders and waist made her figure look more generous. The tops of her budding breasts were exposed, hinting at hidden delights beneath the pale blue satin. She was trembling a little, reaching for Tabitha's hand, but she held her head high.

There was uproar, every man in the room yelling and stamping his feet. An argument broke out near the door as some of them fought for a better view.

'Get on with the auction!' Bergquist demanded, his breath coming hard and fast; like many in the heaving crowd he was obviously aroused by the sight of the girl. When his words didn't bring silence he drew his Colt and sent a bullet zapping into the wooden beam above Lily's head. 'That was no blank. I waited long enough!'

For a second Lily Godine's face flushed with anger. Durgan Vosper had taken no part in the proceedings so far, standing silent and watchful at her side. Now he leant to speak quietly into her ear and the woman pasted the smile back on to her face.

'Shut up and listen good,' she said. 'First, let's get this clear. Whoever makes the highest bid wins sole rights to this beautiful piece of property. And I mean sole rights, I ain't planning on taking her back. You all know how fond I am of our little Melia, and I want what's best for her. Must be a few of you who fancy taking this fine lady home to keep your bed warm, so dig deep and come up with the money. Big heaps of dollar bills, that's what we're looking for.'

At the end of the bar a group of loggers were frantically pooling their pay, and close by the stairs Zeke and four other men from the sawmill were doing the same. Bergquist stood quiet, watching them with contempt.

Durgan Vosper stepped forward, raising his hands for silence. 'Miss Godine has asked me to act as auctioneer, an honour I am happy to accept. Those of you bidding as syndicates, please choose one member to make the bids so we have no confusion. We are starting the bidding at thirty dollars.'

There were groans from some among the crowd and a few growls of discontent, but several men raised their hands and there were shouts of 'forty', 'fifty' and 'sixty-five' before Bergquist bellowed 'a hundred bucks.'

'One hundred twenty,' Zeke responded, bringing a cheer from the men clustered around him.

'One forty,' came from the loggers at the end of the bar. Now at last there was quiet, the sale narrowed down to just three bidders.

'One hundred and fifty,' Bergquist said. Melia stood like a statue but her knuckles were white where she clung to the stair rail. Jarrett wondered if all the colour on her cheeks was rouge; there was something in her wide-eyed stare that suggested the girls might have given her a drink.

'One eighty.' It was the man at the bar. Zeke was whispering with the mill workers, jabbing a finger at one man who was shaking his head.

'Two hundred.' Bergquist grinned. Sure of his victory, he was already moving towards the stairs, barely able to contain his impatience. The men at the bar growled their frustration, and Zeke began a frantic count of the bills he held in his hands.

'Two hundred and fifty dollars.' Jarrett's words dropped into the silence and every pair of eyes swivelled in his direction.

Bergquist stopped in mid stride, turning slowly as if he couldn't believe what he'd heard. He altered course, swaying slightly. The mob separated to let him through. When he was only a yard from Jarrett the marshal halted, legs spread wide, his breathing noisy. 'Back off, Jarrett. The girl's mine. You ain't got no claim here.'

Jarrett gestured towards Vosper, though his eyes held Bergquist's gaze. 'That's not the way an auction works, Marshal. Ask your boss.'

'The bid is with Mr Jarrett,' Vosper agreed, a slight smile playing over his lips, his eyes watchful. 'At two hundred and fifty dollars.'

'Two hundred and sixty.' Bergquist leant forward, giving Jarrett the benefit of breath that stank of stale whiskey.

'Two hundred and seventy,' Jarrett countered evenly.

'Two eighty,' Bergquist was almost too furious to form the words, his jaw working, the pale bloodshot eyes flashing hatred.

'I think it's time to end this,' Jarrett said. 'Three hundred and fifty dollars.'

A hubbub of sound rose around them. Bergquist's bony face was deep red. His right hand crept towards the butt of his six-gun. Jarrett kept still, his right fist still cradling his glass.

'No more bids?' Vosper's voice lifted over the growing chaos of noise.

'He ain't got that much money,' Bergquist ground out. 'He talks big but he's nothin' but a two bit drifter.'

'Money's in my pocket,' Jarrett said. 'You take your hand away from that pistol and I'll be happy to pay Miss Godine right now.'

'Over my dead body,' Bergquist growled. 'Come on, Jarrett, you done nothin' but talk me down since you got here, it's time to show us all what you can do.' He sneered. 'You're yellow, you ain't got the guts to draw on me.'

'That's just the drink talking,' Jarrett observed. 'When you're sober you're not stupid enough to think you can beat me in a gunfight. If you still want to draw on me once you've got that whiskey out of your system then I'm not hard to find, I'll be right down the street at the store.'

Despite being drunk Bergquist was faster than he'd expected, and the gun was already out of the holster when the empty glass hit the floor and shattered. A split second later Jarrett's fist connected hard with the man's exposed throat. If he'd put all his strength into the blow the marshal probably would have died there and then, but

Jarrett pulled the punch at the last moment, knowing he'd done enough. Curling over in pain, retching and choking, Bergquist didn't seem to notice Jarrett taking the Colt from his hand, breaking the gun open and spinning the chamber to spill the shells on to the floor.

'When you're sober,' Jarrett repeated, 'and you're not likely to kill somebody by mistake, then you and me can have another little talk. Reckon if you don't recall what I said there's plenty of friends here to tell you. Right now I figure you'd better get some sleep.' This time he used all his considerable strength, smashing his fist at the point of Bergquist's chin to send him crashing to the floor. The marshal stretched his length all the way to the door and lay still.

'You've done it again,' Vosper came to Jarrett's side. 'I've never known a man so eager to make enemies.'

Jarrett pulled a wad of bills from his pocket and counted out three hundred and fifty dollars. Lily began to check the amount with exaggerated care, but Vosper didn't wait.

'She's all yours.' With a smile he beckoned to Melia. She descended the stairs holding onto the rail as if she wasn't sure of her footing, but when she reached the bottom step she came to them with her head up, shoulders and hips swaying. The mob cheered her on, a hundred voices filling the saloon with comments unfit for a child's ears. Melia flushed but she didn't falter.

Finally she halted in front of Jarrett, the shouts of approval echoing back from the ceiling and walls so loud it hurt the ears. Her heart-shaped face turned to look up at him, with lips parted and eyes alight.

She'd learned her lesson well. In a childlike gesture that mimicked the flagrant invitation of a whore yet was somehow innocent, Melia lifted a hand to encircle the back of his neck and pulled his mouth down onto hers. As their lips met Jarrett felt as if he'd been plunged into a white hot fire.

Pulling free he grabbed the girl's hand and headed for the door, swiping aside a drunken logger who got in his way. He dragged Melia out into the dark street, great waves of laughter and whoops of ribald encouragement erupting behind them.

CHAPTER FIFTEEN

Dawn came to Vosperville as the sun rose clear of the forested mountains. Jarrett leant his back against the wall of the store and breathed deep. The air was cold. Looking down between the crowded buildings he watched the sky lighten over the river and felt a sudden longing for the wide open spaces of his home.

Shrugging the thought aside Jarrett went back inside. He had a job to do. Quietly he passed the locked storeroom door, going through into the yard to pump water over his head, ignoring the instinct that made him glance at the places where a gunman might lie in wait. A man couldn't spend his whole life looking over his shoulder. He touched the scrap of metal concealed under his belt; he didn't think anybody in Vosperville knew why he'd come. If it really was Kate he'd seen the night before he had to be sure it stayed that way.

Filling a can with water he went inside to start making breakfast. There were advantages in running a store, and the coffee from the supply Trig Rawlings had brought smelt good. He carved thick slices of bacon and set out a spread of biscuits along with jars of honey and molasses. Once he had the bacon frying he fetched some eggs and on his way back he turned the key in the storeroom door and rapped on the wood.

'Melia? Coffee's hot.'

There was a deep silence before the door opened. The girl came out with a blanket draped over her shoulders, her thoughts hidden, though the light from the window glinted darkly in her eyes. She walked past him to the stove and poured herself some coffee.

'Aren't you talking to me?' he felt awkward with her.

'Why should I?' she turned her back, heading for the storeroom again, pulling the cover tighter round her body.

'I'm making you breakfast.'

She hesitated then came back. Standing before him she dropped the blanket on the floor. The satin dress hung crumpled and crooked on her shoulders. Tears had run down her cheeks leaving stained rivulets through the remains of powder and paint. She looked like a child who'd been beaten for borrowing her mother's finery.

As she looked up into his eyes there was no trace of the whore she'd pretended to be the night before; the woman born of Melia's brief triumph in the smoky saloon had gone, shrunk back to a child again. She was sober now and there was no joy in her expression.

'When my folks got drowned I couldn't do a thing to help,' she said, her voice flat and cold. 'It seemed like that girl they dragged out of the river wasn't me at all. Like I watched it all happen to some stranger. That's how it was last night. I was letting it all happen, knowing I'd have to go with the marshal, or those old men from the logging camp. I didn't want to care, because I couldn't stop it happening.'

'You don't have to think about that . . .'

She silenced him with a look. 'When you beat the marshal that way I was so happy. I wanted . . . I thought . . .' She dashed angrily at the wetness on her face and stamped her foot. 'Why'd you buy me if you didn't want me?'

Jarrett breathed out long and deep, understanding at last. 'Heck, Melia, it wasn't like that. You're a beautiful girl, any man . . . If you knew . . .' He broke off, recalling the struggle of the night before, the child-woman in the smoky bar, her eyes bright, the tender young body his for the taking. Then the shock of that kiss and the taste of her lips, like a shot of neat moonshine on an empty stomach.

If he'd had more than a single glass of whiskey, or if an older claim on his affections hadn't got in the way, he might not have been able to resist. She'd followed him home in silence, her hand in his like a trusting infant's, then she'd turned to him in the shadowy store, her flesh glowing in the lamplight, the sight and scent of her so inviting. It would have been so easy to forget she was a child.

He had no words to tell her his thoughts. 'You're too young,' he said.

The girl's face brightened, the perfect mouth lifting at the corners. 'But you aren't that old! Why, I've heard the girls talk about Mr Morgen, he must be more'n sixty but he takes two of 'em upstairs every Wednesday night, just like clockwork.'

At that Jarrett laughed aloud, her artless words making him glad he'd listened to his conscience and let her remain a child a little longer. 'I guess there's hope for me yet.'

He turned away from her to serve up the eggs and rescue the bacon before it burnt. 'Come on, eat. Won't grow up if you don't.'

She stared at him doubtfully, inclined to sulk because he'd laughed, then she slid onto the chair and helped herself to a biscuit. 'Folks'll think you're crazy paying a fortune if you don't even want to take me to bed. They'll all be poking fun at me.'

'That's not so. One day you'll make some lucky man

very happy, Melia, but it won't be because he paid money for you.'

'I wanted it to be you,' she said in a small voice, picking at her food. 'I'd like it to be you.'

He looked down at the mop of dark hair and sighed, imagining the soft feel of it beneath his fingers, remembering. 'I've got a girl, Melia. One day maybe she'll even agree to marry me.' Jarrett sat down opposite her and made a start on breakfast. 'Besides, it wasn't my money Lily Godine took last night. If you belong to anyone it's Annie Henderson.'

'Annie?' she stared at him with her mouth hanging open.

Jarrett shrugged. 'She didn't want Bert's winnings from the poker game so I suggested a use for it.'

'So you really didn't want me.' For a moment she was crestfallen, then she looked up at him, eyes wide with sudden fear. 'But what about Marshal Bergquist? He's likely gonna kill you!' She shook her head. 'He won't believe you didn't, that we . . .' She broke off, flushing. 'No good telling him you got another girl.'

'Would you prefer I'd backed down last night?'

She grimaced. 'No.'

Jarrett downed a mouthful of coffee. 'Eat. Then you'd better go and fetch your clothes, you can't walk around dressed like that, the ladies of Vosperville are going to have more than enough to gossip about as it is.'

If there was an unpleasant tingling sensation breathing down the back of his neck Jarrett didn't show it; he stepped out into the street like a man with nothing troubling his mind. It was Sunday and in the absence of a church and preacher the townsfolk had gathered in the open air to say prayers and sing hymns. Jarrett drifted over towards them. Fetching up alongside young Ged Dwyer he traded grins with the youngster and looked over the boy's shoulder to follow the words in his hymn book. The pages had a fringe of black along the top edge as if they'd been scorched in a fire.

Jarrett had barely got his tongue round the second hallelujah when Mrs Dwyer grabbed Ged's arm and pulled the boy away. Gradually the voices of the other singers faded into silence. All eyes were on Jarrett, and not one of them was friendly. The gathering began to break up, men and women pointedly turning their backs, the children twisting round to stare as their parents dragged them away.

Considering these people hadn't had the guts to take Melia out of Lily's keeping a year ago they'd turned pious mighty fast. Jarrett's mouth twisted in a grim smile as he watched them go. He'd get a friendlier reception on board the *Solveg*, and with that in mind he headed towards the wharf.

Then he saw her. The mass of dark hair was held neatly in check under a blue hat, a perfect match for the thick coat she wore against the chill air. She stood outside the marshal's office, head down as she spoke to a small elderly woman. After a moment the two parted and she looked up.

The last thing Jarrett had wanted was to meet Kate in the street where people could see them together. He should have walked away, but he'd never learnt to turn his back on trouble. No doubt the ladies at Miss Jordan's Rooming House already knew why she was in Vosperville, and it wouldn't be long before the whole town heard. He felt suddenly angry. Of all the fool things to do, arriving in this town alone and unprotected. He would have to speak to her, try to make her see sense.

She was coming, threading her way through the dispersing congregation. Jarrett was rooted to the spot.

123

Somewhere deep in his chest a regular thump like the thud of a jackhammer started up, and his annoyance evaporated. It was almost worth risking his neck, just to take a good look at her again.

'Hello Kate.'

The light in her eyes should have warned him, but the sight of her had addled his wits and he didn't see the blow coming until it was too late. Her open palm caught him full across the face, with all her strength behind it.

'Never, ever speak to me again,' she said, her voice low and filled with a cold fury. As she drew her hand back to strike again Jarrett caught hold of her wrist.

'I heard you the first time,' he said, keeping his voice low. 'Are you crazy? You must have heard what happened here, it's not safe for you. Pack your things and get back on that boat.'

'I heard.' There was the glint of tears in her eyes. 'But what I do is none of your business.'

'Maybe that's true. Only if you tell anyone here who I am then my life won't be worth a bent nickel.'

'That's no more than you deserve,' she said, pulling free and turning her back. Even in retreat she was worth looking at, and Jarrett couldn't help admiring the view, until common sense told him it was time to leave. The encounter was over, and half the population of Vosperville had seen it.

A group of lumber workers sniggered from the sidewalk as Jarrett lifted a hand to explore his stinging cheek; Kate had never believed in half measures. But had she heard what he said, and furious as she was, would she keep his secret?

There was a scramble of activity aboard the *Fortune*, but the *Solveg* lay quiet against the wharf, only a solitary sailor standing on her deck. The man nodded when Jarrett asked if the captain was aboard, and before he could set foot on the gangplank Olafsen was there. 'Come, you need a drink.' He grinned. 'And maybe a place to hide, yes?'

'I came to ask for that letter back,' Jarrett said, following the Captain into his cabin. 'The lady isn't in Wilberton any more.'

'I hear. She come to see you.' Olafsen opened the drawer. 'Miss Katherine Sallis,' he read, 'She already give you her answer I think, and she don't wait for the mail.'

'We're old friends,' Jarrett admitted, feeling his face ruefully. 'Can't think why she's so mad at me.'

Olafsen laughed, setting the *Solveg* rocking gently as he stomped across the deck giving free rein to his amusement. 'You say so! When the whole town talk about you and little Melia, and what a good time you had last night. Every man in Vosperville want to be in your shoes, or in your bed.'

Jarrett's mouth dropped open, then snapped shut as he realised Olafsen was right. Not that Kate had any claim on him; he'd asked her to be his wife a dozen times since she turned eighteen, and she'd refused him on every occasion.

'That makes some sort of sense,' he admitted. 'It was Melia I came to talk to you about. I want to get her out of town, somewhere Bergquist can't reach her.'

'Better you both leave,' the Captain growled. 'Vosper soon connect you with this woman, and with her brother. Then you have big trouble.'

With a sigh Jarrett accepted the drink Olafsen offered. 'I've already got that. Besides, maybe I'm not the only one. Taking my side against Vosper may not have been a wise move.'

'I tell the truth, no more,' Olafsen said.

There was the sound of voices from on deck, then the

patter of light feet coming down the companionway. Melia burst in on them, her face flushed, a small untidy parcel in her arms, and the sailor who'd been on watch pounding furiously along right behind her.

CHAPTER SIXTEEN

'I didn't know where you'd gone, I was real worried,' Melia said breathlessly, slipping out from under the sailor's hands and running to Jarrett. 'You have to get out of town.'

'I tell him that,' Olafsen said, dismissing the deckhand with a gesture.

'Bergquist won't try anything,' Jarrett said. 'Not once he's sober.'

'It isn't just Bergquist.' Melia gave up on Jarrett and turned to the captain with her appeal. 'The girls say Vosper's men are planning to kill him.'

'Vosper offered me a job,' Jarrett reminded her. 'And time to think about taking it.'

'He thought you were just another hired gun like Hook and the others, but he's changed his mind. Last night Ramirez and Felipe were bragging about how they'd leave you for the coyotes. Mr Vosper laughed and said you could afford a funeral. He said selling the store would give you a real big send off.'

Jarrett looked down into her flushed face and smiled. 'I appreciate the warning. You don't have to worry, if those two rats try anything I'll be ready for them.'

'No! There's time for you to get away.'

'I'm going nowhere,' Jarrett said.

She stamped her foot at him, her face flushing with anger. 'You've got no more sense than Hoby, and you're going to end up dead just like he did!'

Captain Olafsen nodded. 'She is right,' he said solemnly. 'I think it bad for you to stay here, my friend. Vosper knows you are not a rascal like those men of his. I think it better you leave.'

'I can't,' Jarrett said. 'There's something I still have to do in Vosperville.'

'No good to risk your neck,' Olafsen growled. 'Tomorrow you come aboard and we go to Wilberton. My men and me, we return with *Solveg* soon, no matter what Vosper say. We bring you back, we help with those things to do.'

'No.' Jarrett met Olafsen's eyes. 'I appreciate the offer, but I'm not leaving.'

'Make him go,' Melia said suddenly.

'How I do that?' Olafsen looked down at her, his mouth twitching. 'You think I send my men in the night, knock him out with a warming pan maybe?'

The girl flushed. 'He shouldn't have told you about that. Anyway if you're his friend then you'd do it, to stop him getting himself killed.'

'I'm not planning on dying just yet,' Jarrett said. 'And I'm better off without that kind of friendship, my head's still sore.' He turned back to the captain, reaching in his pocket for a handful of dollar bills. 'If there's a spare berth I'd be grateful if you'd see Melia safe down river. And she'll need a place to say in Wilberton.'

'No.' Melia's face was suddenly ashen. 'I'm not going on any boat. I don't want to be drowned like my ma and pa.'

'*Solveg* the best boat on this river.' Olafsen was offended. 'A hundred storms we go through. She never take water. Come aboard after dark. Bergquist never know where you are.'

Melia stared at him blankly then turned to look at Jarrett, terror in her eyes.

'I'll be a whole lot safer with you gone,' Jarrett told her.

Although the moon shone brightly over the river it was pitch dark below the *Solveg*'s decks. Somewhere forward there was noise and laughter but here it was quiet. Captain Olafsen held the lantern high and ushered Melia past him.

'This place for you.' He showed them a tiny cabin with black wooden walls and a narrow bunk heaped with blankets. 'Once we clear Vosperville I fetch you. I tell my men if they touch you I kill them.'

'You'll be fine,' Jarrett said, patting the girl clumsily on the shoulder. 'I'll come to Wilberton soon as I can, maybe even on the *Fortune*. It's only for a few days.'

She nodded dumbly, putting her bundle down on the bunk and collapsing beside it, her body slumped in misery.

'Good, you sleep now.' Olafsen beamed and steered Jarrett back into the narrow companionway. 'Come my friend, we have a drink before you go.'

Trig Rawlings sat in the captain's cabin waiting for them, a half empty bottle in his hand, two full ones on the table in front of him. He staggered to his feet. 'You comin' down river with us, Rick? Be real nice to have company.'

'No,' Jarrett said, 'just came to wish you a good trip. Seems I didn't need to bother, reckon the captain's looking after you pretty well.'

'I like a man who drinks rum,' Olafsen said, taking the bottle to refill Rawlings glass then pouring generous measures for himself and Jarrett. 'He know what is good.'

'I prefer whiskey,' Jarrett remarked, but he tossed off the drink without further argument.

'This stuff warms you up from the inside,' Rawlings said

indistinctly. 'Lights a fire that sets on top of your belly real cosy.'

Jarrett sat down beside him. 'By the look of you that's quite a blaze. Trouble is by morning it'll feel like your head's full of cinders.'

'When a man offers you a drink it ain't manners to turn him down. Come on, you both got some catchin' up to do.'

Two empty bottles rolled slowly across the deck. Trig Rawlings snored rhythmically, his head resting against Jarrett's boot. 'Time I was going,' Jarrett said, standing up and pausing a moment, checking that the world was only shifting because of the motion of the boat beneath his feet. Rawlings rolled over and settled down again, a smile on his face.

Captain Olafsen looked up at Jarrett. 'No. We go to Wilberton.' He too pushed upright, clinging to the table for support. 'Not good for you to stay.'

Jarrett smiled. 'You did your best Captain, but I'm a whole lot closer to sober than you are, and I don't think you're fit to make a fight of it. You can tell Melia you tried.'

'Nobody drink rum that way.' With an effort Olafsen focused on Jarrett's face. 'Only me. How you do that?'

'Kept changing glasses with Trig here when you weren't looking.' He nudged the unconscious man with his toe. 'When he's nursing that sore head in the morning you'd best apologize for me.' Picking up his rifle Jarrett headed out of the cabin. 'I'll see you in a week or two, Captain, have a good trip.'

Olafsen blinked at him, then he took an ancient watch from his pocket and stared at it. 'Coffee,' he roared. 'Somebody fetch me coffee!'

Jarrett strode to the end of the wharf and climbed down so he could reach clear water, putting the

Winchester on a step where it was close to hand. He stooped in the dim light of the setting moon to sluice water over his head, chasing away the effects of the drink. When his head felt clear he hunkered down on the step beside his gun with his arms wrapped close around him for warmth, and waited for the sky to lighten. At last the lanterns aboard the *Solveg* were extinguished, there was a bustle of activity as the crew bent to their work, the men's breath steaming in the cold. Captain Olafsen's voice sounded loud and clear and a minute later the warps were cast off.

A handful of townsfolk were there to see the boat draw away from its berth. They waved to their loved ones standing on deck, wrapped up against the dawn chill. 'Bye Melia,' Jarrett muttered. He watched the *Solveg*'s departure with a lightening heart; whatever happened to him the girl would be out of Bergquist's way. With the last fifty dollars of Annie's money in his pocket Olafsen had promised to find her a decent place to stay in Wilberton until Jarrett sent word that it was safe for her to return.

Once the boat was well on her way the small crowd began to leave the wharf, and Jarrett stepped up to join them. One man turned away hurriedly as he approached, hunched in his black morning coat as if he was afraid of being recognized. It was Crump, the undertaker. As Jarrett started after him he picked up speed, casting frightened looks over his shoulder. When Crump ducked through a gap in the wall of the half-finished sawmill Jarrett smiled to himself and lengthened his stride, going around to the other side to intercept the fleeing man.

'Now if that's not a pleasant surprise,' Jarrett drawled, grabbing Crump's shoulder as he peered warily out of his hiding place. The undertaker froze in shock, his jaw dropping open. 'I've been wanting to have another word with you.'

131

'I've got nothing to say,' Crump said, his voice rising to a frantic squeak. 'Not here, please. Somebody might see.'

'Where?' Jarrett tightened his grip.

'I have to drive to the cemetery and mark out a new plot,' Crump's voice trembled. 'I'll be there in half an hour. If you take the south road and work uphill through the trees nobody will see you.'

'If you aren't there . . .'

'I'll come, I swear it.' Crump nodded his head frantically. 'I'll be there.'

Jarrett let him go and watched him scuttle away. Then he turned towards the south road and started walking. Crump was only a few minutes behind him, driving a single-horse rig. The undertaker climbed down, tied the horse to the fence and led the way to a hollow above the burying ground.

'You want me to tell you about Father Martin,' he said.

'That's right,' Jarrett replied, 'everybody knows his death was no accident.'

Crump's mouth opened and closed a couple of times. 'If they find out I've told you they'll kill me.'

'Vosper's men? They might not get the chance. I'm sick of folk in this town giving me the run around. If you don't come clean I'll carry you down to the river and see how well you can swim with a log tied to your feet.' Jarrett reached for a hold on Crump's collar. 'Never thought about it before, who does the burying if the undertaker's dead? Maybe I'll find out.'

'No, please!' Crump made a feeble attempt to pull away. 'I don't know who killed him. What I know isn't going to help you much.'

'Try me,' Jarrett said.

Crump swallowed hard. 'It was when I was laying out the body. He'd been quite badly burnt, there wasn't much I could do for him except peel off what was left of his clothes and wrap him up. But a heavy piece of wood must have fallen across his back because the flesh there was hardly touched. That's when I noticed it.'

'Noticed what?'

'The bullet wound. It was fresh. Only a little hole, a small calibre pistol probably.'

'Like that fancy little derringer Felipe carries.'

'I don't know. I suppose so. I daren't examine the wound closely, there were people helping me, and I didn't want them to see what I'd found. Some folk were spoiling for trouble, it would have meant more bloodshed.'

'More trade for you,' Jarrett said coldly. 'I'm surprised you're so squeamish. Tell me the rest.'

'There was hardly any blood. From the position of the wound I'd guess the shot hit the heart. Father Martin was probably dead before he ever fell into the fire.'

Jarrett's thoughts were grim as he went back to the store, but as he reached to put the key into the lock he returned to the present with a jolt. A long splinter of wood hung down from beside the shattered lock, and as he touched it the door swung away from him.

Thrusting the door wide Jarrett flattened himself against the wall, the Winchester cocked. The crash of wood on wood echoed loud but there was only silence within. He eased forward half a step at a time, eyes slitted against the darkness, ears straining.

It was the smell that told him. Over the last few days he'd grown used to the compound scent of coffee, pepper, oil and a dozen other things, but now there was something else, a powerful odour that made his heart quicken its beat. Going in fast, he stopped as he noticed the pathetic bundle that lay against the counter. Melia's belongings that she'd packed for her trip on the *Solveg*. They should-n't be here and nor should she, but her fear of the river must have brought her back, she'd sneaked ashore while he was drinking Olafsen's rum.

Knowing what he was going to find, his mouth a thin hard line, Jarrett moved through into the kitchen, leading with the Winchester, the butt firm against his shoulder, yet certain he'd find no enemy inside.

He was right. Only Melia was there.

Jarrett had watched men kick out their lives at the end of a rope, more than he liked to remember. He'd tended a friend who took two days dying after he'd been shot in the gut. Then there were those he'd personally despatched to Hades; he'd made a point of not keeping count. Never once had the sight of death made him sick to his stomach. Not until now.

Melia lay on the ruins of her dowdy brown dress, now darkened with splashes of her blood. Her once beautiful face was blotched and swollen; when he'd finished with her Bergquist must have tightened those long bony hands of his around her throat. Only the cloud of dark hair was unsullied, spread like a halo around that ruined perfection.

134

CHAPTER SEVENTEEN

The axe splintered the door of the marshal's office like match wood, glass from the windows showering to the ground with a crash. Jarrett's second blow shattered the lock and the door burst open. He let the polished shaft slip from his hands, reaching to grab the Winchester that was slung across his shoulder.

'Bergquist!' Too mad for caution he ploughed across the office to the rooms behind. A jug of coffee bubbled on the stove and a rear door stood open on to the yard behind the Double Eagle. Returning to the office Jarrett noted the empty space on the gun rack where the marshal's shotgun should have been. Back in the street he picked up the discarded axe. 'I'd say it's still pretty sharp,' he said, tossing it to the bemused logger who'd been on his way to the smithy behind the sawmills when Jarrett stopped him.

A crowd was gathering outside the saloon, brought by the noise of his assault on the marshal's office. Nobody got in Jarrett's way as he charged through the swing doors. The bar was empty, the smell of stale smoke and drink hanging over the litter of dirty glasses and cigarette butts from the previous night.

'Bergquist!' Jarrett started up the stairs two at a time. Before he was halfway the screen at the top swung aside and the red-haired Tabitha appeared.

'He ain't here.' She said. 'You crazy, bustin' up the town?'

'I've got reason,' Jarrett said, moving on towards her, 'Where's Bergquist? The sonofabitch killed Melia.'

The girl flinched. 'Melia? He wouldn't do that . . .'

'No? You think you know the kind of man he is? Treats you real kind and gentle, I bet. He never put his hands around your neck and kept on squeezing until you couldn't breathe, until he'd strangled the life out of you.'

'He ain't here,' she spoke as if the words alone could choke her. 'I swear it. Come take a look.'

Jarrett ran the rest of the way upstairs. A handful of women spilled out of the rooms, but they made no attempt to stop him as he checked that the girl was telling the truth. He went back to her. 'Where would he go?'

Her pale eyes met his and she shivered as if a sudden chill caught her. 'If he knows you're lookin' for him he'll be hidin' out someplace. With the boss maybe.'

It figured. Bergquist could be mighty brave with a bunch of hired guns to back him up. The crowd on the street split to let Jarrett pass, and he could feel their eyes on his back as he made his way up the hill. Outside Vosper's imposing mansion a figure slouched against one of the fancy columns that flanked the front door.

'Lookin' for somebody?' Jude asked insolently. 'Mr Vosper's busy.'

'Where's Bergquist?'

'I wouldn't know.'

'Then let's go and find somebody who does,' Jarrett said curtly. 'Your boss will do.' He lifted the Winchester and worked the action. 'Now.'

Jude rapped on the door and it was opened by a manservant in a dark grey jacket. The youngster elbowed past him and led the way into a huge hall lit by chandeliers hanging high above a polished floor. Jarrett followed Jude to a smaller room, and as they approached he could hear voices, one of them Vosper's smooth cultured tone, the other lighter and uncomfortably familiar.

Pushing Jude aside from the doorway Jarrett found himself in an office dominated by the large steel safe in one corner. Kate Sallis was seated by the window, with Durgan Vosper hovering attentively at her side.

'Mr Jarrett.' Vosper's tone was light, but his eyes showed his anger. 'I trust you have a good reason for forcing your way into my house.'

'Mr Jarrett isn't renowned for his manners,' Kate said tightly, a frown appearing between her brows.

'Obviously not,' Vosper said, 'Forgive me, Miss Sallis,' he returned his attention to Kate. 'I'd heard you two were acquainted.'

'The lady's no friend of mine,' Jarrett said, moving round so he could keep the Winchester on Vosper without the risk of Kate getting in the line of fire.

'There's no mystery.' She ignored Jarrett and addressed herself solely to Vosper. 'It was a long time ago. Mr Jarrett took advantage of me when I was young and inexperienced. He hoped to marry me and get his hands on my father's money. When his plan failed he robbed me and moved on.' A faint flush rose to her cheeks. 'I'm ashamed of my public display of temper, you'll have to forgive me. Coming so soon after the news about my brother's death, seeing this man again was too much of a shock.'

Jarrett's fingers relaxed minutely on the butt of the Winchester. 'So that's why you're here,' he said. 'Came as a shock to me too, seeing the name in the cemetery.'

'I came to visit my brother and found he'd been dead since last fall,' she said, keeping her gaze on the floor at her feet. 'Before I leave I'm taking comfort from the tributes of the people who knew him.' Then at last she looked up at him. He couldn't read the thought in her eyes; beneath the fury something else lurked in the depths. 'How fortunate you only arrived recently, or I might have thought his death wasn't an accident.'

'I never had anything against him,' Jarrett said.

She stared blankly at him then looked away. 'Mr Vosper, you'll excuse me, but if you have business with this man perhaps I should leave.'

'No please, we must talk further. Although I have to confess I've never been a regular churchgoer I got to know your brother quite well. It's a matter of deep regret to me that I wasn't present when the accident occurred, there's a chance the tragedy might have been averted.'

He picked up a bell from the desk and rang it to bring the servant. 'Bernard, Miss Sallis and I will take tea in the drawing-room.'

As the man nodded and left, Vosper escorted Kate to the door and bowed over her hand with old fashioned courtesy. 'I'll join you in a few minutes. Jude, keep Miss Sallis company until I come.'

Jude flashed a mean look at Jarrett then offered Kate his arm.

'Thank you.' She smiled at Vosper over her shoulder, sweeping coldly past Jarrett.

A moment later there was the click of a door closing down the hall and Vosper turned back to Jarrett. 'Well?'

'I'm looking for Bergquist.'

'The marshal?' Vosper raised his eyebrows in mock astonishment. 'What makes you think he'd be here?'

'I went to the Double Eagle, they said he'd run to the boss.'

'And exactly what do you want with him?' Vosper's gaze strayed to the Winchester.

'Not long ago he accused me of murder,' Jarrett said

grimly. 'I'd like to return the favour. Only this time there's a body.'

'The girl.' It wasn't a question. 'If you'd never interfered she'd still be alive.'

'Maybe.' Jarrett was grim. 'I'll ask you one more time, Vosper. Where is he?'

'Not here. You misunderstood what the whores told you, Jarrett. Lily Godine is the boss. You'll find him hiding under her skirts.'

Jarrett gave a slight shake of his head. 'He's not at the Double Eagle.'

'Not in the cat house perhaps. Lily has rooms above the lawyer's office. You won't have noticed the door in the recess at the end of the landing. She also has a private entrance through the back yard.'

Vosper looked at him questioningly. 'When the post of town marshal comes vacant it's yours, if you want it.'

'I'd sooner roast in Hell,' Jarrett said evenly.

'A fool to the last. My men will come with you to find Bergquist. You won't mind?'

'Do I get a choice?'

'None.' Vosper's eyes were cold and hard. 'If you won't work for me there's no room for you in this town, Jarrett.'

There was a sound from the doorway and Jarrett swung round. Ramirez, Felipe and Brossman stood in the hall. He glanced back at Vosper. 'One thing,' he said. 'Call it a last request. They don't interfere until I've dealt with Bergquist.'

'Of course,' Vosper said mockingly. 'Justice must be done. Our marshal overstepped the mark, I have no objection to letting you get rid of him for me. You hear that, gentlemen, a fair contest. After that it's open season.' He laughed. 'Goodbye Mr Jarrett.'

The streets were deserted as if folks knew there was a showdown coming. It was like the quiet before a hurricane. They locked their doors and shutters as if that would shelter them from the storm, only once Jarrett was dead nothing would have changed; Vosper and his hired guns would go on terrorizing the town, and the decent folk would move out, or turn their faces to the wall so they didn't see what was happening.

Bergquist was just enough of a coward to back-shoot him from the upper floor of the saloon; Jarrett took to the sidewalk. There was no chance he'd walk away from this, not with three men waiting for him once he'd dealt with the marshal, but he wanted to be sure and send Melia's killer to the devil first.

Brossman shouldered past Jarrett as they reached the saloon. 'Reckon I'll go make sure he's there,' he said. 'Mr Vosper wants a fair fight, be a real shame if you get yourself shot soon as you walk through the door.'

Jarrett didn't argue. Bergquist stood at the far end of the counter, his shotgun lying before him. There was a film of sweat on the bony face, but he smiled when he saw Jarrett's escort.

'You got company, Jarrett. That make up for losing your little whore?'

'If I had the time I'd make you pay for what you did, Bergquist, inch by inch.' Jarrett walked to the opposite end of the bar and put the Winchester down on the stained wood, its muzzle pointing at the marshal's chest. He let his hands fall to his sides. 'But I just have to hope you'll fry in Hell. Why kill her?'

'She was a noisy little bitch.' Bergquist's fingers explored a bloody scratch on his cheek. 'Fought like a cat too. Not worth three hundred and fifty bucks. How come you never took her yourself, Jarrett? Maybe Lily was right, you ain't much of a man.'

'She was a child,' Jarrett said, noting the way Felipe and

Brossman flanked the door, while Ramirez had moved across to stand by the stairs. Jude had come to join the party and stood silhouetted in the doorway. If they followed Vosper's orders they wouldn't shoot until he and Bergquist had fought. After that . . . With a little luck he'd take Felipe before he died, so Martin could rest easy in his grave. A bubble of wry amusement ran through him. It looked like they'd all end up in the same cemetery.

'Enough talk.' Jarrett fixed his eyes on the tall man. 'Your shotgun against the Winchester. At this range you don't have to be accurate. All you need is the guts to pick up that gun and fire.'

Bergquist sent a hasty glance at Ramirez. The Indian grinned and nodded. The marshal seemed reassured.

'You got religion, Jarrett?' The long bony face contorted into a leering smile. 'Heaven an' Hell, that's the choice ain't it? Reckon you'll be seein' the little slut again real soon. Or maybe there's a special place for whores.'

'Time to die, Bergquist.' Jarrett's voice was dangerously quiet. 'Ramirez, why don't you give us the word.'

The man nodded. 'Sure. I'll count. You pick up the guns on three.' He hooked his thumbs into his belt, watching the two men at opposite ends of the bar. 'One. Two . . .'

The shotgun was already coming up to Bergquist's shoulder, his eyes squinting as he prepared to sight down the barrel. There was no time for Jarrett to lift his own gun; at such close range the scatter of shot would disable him even if it didn't kill him outright. He'd known Bergquist would cheat, and he was ready. He cocked the Winchester where it lay, slamming his left hand down on the butt to keep it steady. Then he put his trigger finger through the guard and exerted exactly the right amount of pressure.

Everything happened at once, time slowing. Triumph

written clear on his bony features, Bergquist froze as a small hole appeared on the front of his vest. He toppled forward and the shotgun bellowed, gouging a lump out of the bar counter, sending a shower of splinters flying. Vosper's men had all drawn their handguns, they were moving forward, closing the range. At the same instant pain exploded through Jarrett's body. He couldn't figure out what had happened. Nobody else had fired.

The Winchester had bucked back into him. It still lay on the bar but it had turned itself around. His right hand rested over the trigger but the left had fallen to his side, and as he tried to lift it a tearing agony that started at his shoulder ripped through him. Only then did Jarrett realise that the recoil had torn his arm from the shoulder socket.

The four gunmen were closing in. Death was only a breath away.

'Hold your fire!' Felipe knocked Jude's arm so his shot went wide then he leapt forward and took the Winchester from Jarrett's unresisting grasp. Through a red haze Jarrett saw Bergquist collapse onto the floor, his sightless eyes already glazing over.

Bringing his malevolent face close up to Jarrett's, Felipe grinned, reaching out to grip his injured arm. Jarrett clamped his teeth together to prevent the scream that started in the back of his throat. Only a low growl of pain escaped him.

'What we waitin' for?' Brossman demanded.

'Vosper don't say there's no hurry,' Felipe said, licking his lips. 'We can have ourselves some fun.'

'That's enough!' Lily Godine stood on the landing with a shotgun in her hands. 'Mo, get out here!'

The mournful barman came slinking from the back room.

'Go fetch the undertaker,' Lily ordered.

'While you're about it, tell him he's got another customer at the store,' Jarrett said harshly, holding down the pain while he looked up at the woman. 'You know Bergquist murdered Melia?'

'The little fool should've known when she was well off.' Lily glanced dispassionately at Bergquist's body. 'Go play your games someplace else, boys, you made enough mess already.'

CHAPTER EIGHTEEN

Waves of pain threatened to send Jarrett down into a black swirling hole. He struggled to remain conscious, vaguely aware that he was being hustled up the street, finding himself somehow standing in front of Chalky White's barn. Brossman was beside him grinning widely, a huge hand clamped onto his right arm. As he was pulled towards the door Jarrett made one desperate attempt to resist, twisting free and slicing the side of his boot down Brossman's leg.

'You learn the hard way, mister,' the big man growled, the smile disappearing and his fist coming hard against the back of Jarrett's neck, the blow propelling him to the dusty floor of the barn. He took the brunt of the fall on his right shoulder but still the force of the landing shot fiery pain down his left side and he had to bite down hard to avoid crying out.

There was a powerful scent of rat, sour in his nostrils; very apt. He was up against four of the meanest rats he'd ever met, with a dislocated shoulder and not a hope in hell of any of the townsfolk coming to help him out. Whatever Felipe might think, for him the next few minutes weren't going to be a heap of fun.

Felipe stood over him, an unpleasant smile on his face. 'You think we kill you quick if we get mad at you?' He bent

144

down and took hold of Jarrett's left hand, giving it a gentle tug, watching his victim's face with greedy eyes. 'Maybe you got somethin' you want to say?'

The world tilted and shuddered. The pain took Jarrett's breath away and it was a while before he could speak. 'Was it you that shot Father Martin?' He asked at last.

'Sure. Mr Vosper, he get tired of that holy man. He want the church out of the way.' His grin widened. 'We find this pretty little statue, an' we throw it into the flames. The priest, he go to fetch it. Then I shoot.' He shrugged. 'An act of mercy. A quick death, no? Maybe soon you envy him.'

'You filthy little runt,' Jarrett tried to push himself up but collapsed as Felipe gave his arm another tug.

'You think you can talk to me that way,' Felipe said softly, letting go of him and standing up. 'We teach you some manners now.' He stamped his boot down on Jarrett's arm and the world dissolved into a fiery ball of pain.

'An' that's for Hook,' Ramirez said, aiming a kick at his back.

Jarrett rolled and came up against a pair of legs, probably Jude's. The red hot agony that was spreading from his dislocated shoulder into the rest of his body made it impossible to think straight. It was hard to force himself to keep moving, but he slammed upwards with his right fist, catching the youngster behind the knee and hearing a grunt of pain as Jude staggered.

It went strangely quiet. The expected reprisal didn't come and all Jarrett could hear was the labouring of his own breath. He blinked a couple of times, trying to clear the mist from his eyes, and saw what had caused the momentary lull in his punishment.

Chalky White was coming down the ladder that led from the loft, the bullet head bare atop the short heavy body. The thread of hope that had woven itself through Jarrett's mind untangled and left him once more alone, his life about to be permanently undone. A dozen of the townspeople might have taken on Vosper's men, Jarrett thought inconsequentially, but alone this old man would be as much help as his sway backed mare.

'Get out,' Ramirez said.

'I was tryin' to sleep,' Chalky replied, keeping his gaze averted from Jarrett where he lay on the floor. 'You folks won't mind me goin' to the saloon where I can have a drink in peace?'

Felipe laughed. 'What's the matter, you got a weak stomach?'

'Strong enough when it's full of whiskey.' Ramirez said, grinning.

Brossman pulled the Indian aside so Chalky could pass. 'Let him go. Don't want to keep a man from his drink.'

Chalky hitched forward a couple of paces. 'Don't you go disturbing my horse,' he grumbled. As he put out a hand towards the mare's head, he seemed to stumble.

Jarrett wouldn't have believed the old man could move with such speed. One second he was a stout slightly stooped figure about to hitch himself out of the door, the next he'd swept up the pitchfork that was leaning against the stall and thrust the end of the handle hard into Ramirez's belly, knocking him down. Chalky reversed the tool so fast it was a blur.

Ramirez lay frozen in fear, staring in disbelief at the twin points digging into him, just at the base of his ribs, with Chalky leaning his weight on the wooden shaft.

'You know,' the old man said, only slightly out of breath, as Brossman and Felipe both reached for their sidearms, 'when you shoot a man he falls forward. Don't make sense, but I seen it a dozen times or more. Guess maybe you boys have too. So unless you want me to send

your friend here to the devil, you'd best not think of takin'
that shot.'

Careful to move wide around Felipe, Jarrett pushed
himself clear then rose shakily to his feet. 'Didn't figure
there was a man with guts left in this town,' he said.

'Might not be for long,' Chalky replied, not taking his
eyes from their adversaries. 'The three of you better drop
those belts unless you want to see this heap of horse shit
spitted ready for the griddle. Figure he'd be kinda tough
an' greasy, so let's not waste the firewood.'

Jude's gun belt dropped. Brossman looked sidelong at
Felipe and began slowly working at the buckle of his own
belt. Felipe hadn't moved a muscle. Watching his face,
Jarrett saw the exact moment when the little man decided
to let Ramirez die. In the flicker of an eye his hand was on
its way to the Colt hidden below the filthy blanket that
swathed his scrawny body.

Screaming this time at the agony shooting through him
Jarrett flung himself at Jude's gun belt where it lay on the
floor, dragging the .45 from the holster and firing as his
body hit the dirt, taking aim without thought. Through
tears of pain he saw the shot find its mark. Felipe toppled,
his face an unrecognizable mask of blood, the bullet from
his Colt burying itself harmlessly in the earth floor.

Brossman made his play at the same time, but the
bubbling shriek of Ramirez's dying checked him for a
breath, and Chalky was a moving target, dropping on top
of Ramirez's twitching body. The giant got off two rounds,
the sound battering at Jarrett's ears as it blended into the
echo of the shot that had killed Felipe, a crashing roll
bouncing off the solid wooden walls.

It was hard to say which of them killed the big man.
Jarrett's bullet took him in the head and Chalky, drawing
Ramirez's gun with his left hand and firing at a range of
no more than four feet, plugged him in the chest. The

barn no longer smelt of rat. Powder smoke and dust mingled with the metallic scent of hot blood. Only Jude remained standing, his slack mouth open, his hands dangling at his sides as he stared at the carnage around him.

Jarrett didn't want to stand up again but it was necessary. Gritting his teeth he ignored the burning torment exploding from his left shoulder with each beat of his pulse. As he drew a bead on Jude's head with the youngster's own gun Jude began to shake, lifting his trembling hands as if to plead for his life. The sound of running water trickled into the renewed silence as a dark patch appeared down the front of his pants.

'If I ever see you again,' Jarrett grated, 'I'll take your head off your shoulders with a blunt knife.'

'Same goes for me,' Chalky White said, breathing hard.

White faced, the youngster looked from one man to the other then turned and fled. Once he was out in the street he paused and looked back. 'You'll be the ones leaving,' he shouted shrilly. 'I'm going to tell Mr Vosper. You better get out quick.' Before Jarrett could take aim he took to his heels again, disappearing from view.

'Shouldn't have let him go.' Chalky was still on the ground, rubbing his knee.

'You hurt?' Jarrett asked, suddenly concerned. His own legs felt like he'd been hamstrung and each move sent a message of agony jangling from his torn shoulder to the rest of his body.

'No.' Chalky waved him away and stood up slowly. 'It's just the rheumatics. I'm sixty six years old, son, far too ancient for this kinda game.'

'If that was true I'd be dead, or close to it,' Jarrett said. 'Where d'you learn to fight like that?'

'I was fightin' for the Union when you was suppin' your ma's milk.' He straightened up, groaning. 'An' I'll be payin' for this for days.'

'We may not have days,' Jarrett reminded him. 'Vosper's not going to be pleased when he finds out we've removed three of his men.'

'Removed.' Chalky chuckled. 'Sure like your way with words, son.' He looked at the slaughter they'd wrought between them. 'Exactly what were you tryin' to do, start a war all on your own?'

Jarrett sighed, carefully. 'I got so mad about Melia I lost my head.'

'Melia?'

'Bergquist killed her.'

The old man's face froze in shock. 'He killed that kid? Sonofabitch! Guess that's reason enough for tackling Bergquist, but where did these three come in?'

'Vosper didn't like me turning him down when he offered me the job of marshal.' Jarrett managed a thin smile, though there was no humour in it. 'They were meant to finish me quick, only when I put my shoulder out Felipe couldn't resist having a little fun before he plugged me.' He winced, gritting his teeth; now the fight was over there was too much time to think about the pain. 'Quite a party.'

Chalky snorted. 'Some folks got a mighty strange idea of entertainment. Sit down there and lean against the wall an' I'll fix that arm for you.'

'You sure you know what you're doing?'

'Shut up and let an old man think.' He took hold of Jarrett, one hand at the wrist, the other at the elbow. 'There's a trick to this, do it real slow, and get it right first time. Hold on, son.' He lifted the arm out straight then pulled the elbow across.

In front of Jarrett's eyes the shafts of dusty sunlight wavered and swayed, becoming lines of red pain. He clenched his teeth and tried to hang on to the sight of

Chalky's round face, eyes narrowed in concentration. A few more agonizing seconds passed then there was a crunch from his shoulder as the joint clicked back into place. The world steadied and Jarrett let out his breath. He stared down at his hand and flexed it. 'You did it,' he said incredulously.

'Yeah. When we was fightin' the rebs at Manassas a man got himself too close to the mouth of a field piece and the blast hit him. Ball missed, but he got both his arms blown clear out of their sockets. Wasn't a scratch on him but he was screamin' so loud we couldn't hear the gunfire. Would never have believed it if I hadn't seen it myself. Only a kid he was, 'bout eighteen. Came from Cincinnati. I took him to the surgeon and watched him put them joints straight, and within a minute the kid was on his feet and raring to get back to the fight. He died of the fever a few months later at Chickahominy.'

Chalky stirred Ramirez's body with his foot. 'How do we keep from gettin' lynched for this? Vosper's likely to call out every man from the lumber camp and track us down. Reckon we'll need ourselves a miracle.'

'Maybe not. You heard what Felipe said. He fired the shot but it was Vosper who wanted Father Martin dead.'

'Figured that might be why you was here.'

'A part of it, anyway. Felipe won't be shooting anyone else in the back, but I still want the man who gave him his orders.'

'You won't get Vosper to stand up and face you with a gun in his hand,' Chalky warned. 'Men like that don't do their own dirty work.'

'Then we'll find some other way.' Jarrett stared out at the empty street. He had the beginnings of an idea hatching in his head, but he'd have to move fast. 'You reckon now we've cleared the air folks in town might see things a little different?'

Chalky looked doubtful. 'Don't figure on no heroics.'

'If you say so.' Jarrett grinned at him. 'You stuck your neck out once, are you willing to do it again?'

'Hell, why not,' Chalky said. 'I'm sick of actin' like some frightened old maid, life on Vosper's terms ain't worth livin'.'

'Good. Then you'd best make yourself scarce while I hightail it out of town. Come on, I'll tell you the plan while I saddle my horse.'

CHAPTER NINETEEN

Jarrett pushed hard along the southbound trail until the forest began to close in around him, then he wheeled the bay and looked back. There were four riders on their way from Vosper's house to the town, while down at the saw mill more were assembling. The two groups joined outside the Double Eagle, and Vosper led his men thundering out of town on Jarrett's tail. A solitary horseman broke away from the group, heading north towards the lumber camp.

It was a crazy ride, the ground treacherous with ice and mud, but Jarrett's bay was eager to run and Vosper's private posse couldn't close the gap. By the time he reached the spot where he'd descended from the high trail the day Bert Henderson died, the pursuers weren't in sight. Jarrett faced the bay at the steep slope. The horse snorted its disapproval but scrambled desperately up the precipitous incline to the safety of level ground above.

Jarrett pulled up, listening for the sounds of the riders below. Dragging the Winchester from its holster he took aim as the men came into view. He planted the first shot just in front of the leading horse. The animal shied and bolted down towards the river, unseating its rider.

A couple of minutes later another of Vosper's followers drove his horse at the steep slope, the animal's hoofs clattering frantically on the loose rock as the man raked its sides with his spurs. With easy precision Jarrett sent a bullet slapping into a sapling under the horse's nose, and it flung itself away and came crashing down on its side, trapping the rider's leg as it rolled over and back onto the trail. The horse stood up and shook itself, but the rider lay sprawled in the mud and didn't move.

Jarrett fired twice more; even when they were sure he'd gone, only those who were well-mounted would risk the slope. Vosper was sure to make it on his black Arabian, but Jarrett was gambling on getting no more than four men on his tail. The rest must turn back or ride on to the junction at the Chinchawa, which meant they would be at least twenty minutes behind.

Jarrett started back towards town. When he checked briefly only Vosper and two of his men were following. Seeing Jarrett they pushed their horses to a raking gallop and he wheeled to urge his tiring mount to its limit. 'Just keep me out of range,' he said, leaning low and running a hand down the sweating neck, 'and there's a sack of oats with your name on it.'

He burst out into the open, close to Vosper's house, and steadied the horse as it hit fresh ruts in the mud. It looked as if Chalky had been busy. Jarrett dragged the bay's head around and pulled up outside the fancy stone portico.

The front door opened and Chalky White appeared. 'We're ready,' he said.

Jarrett lit down. 'Any trouble?'

'Nope. Couple of men Vosper left behind hightailed it, an' the men off the *Fortune* are gettin' drunk in the Double Eagle.' Chalky led the way inside, bending to pick something up from behind the door. It was a torch, an oil-soaked rag tied round one end.

Following the older man to the office where Vosper had met him that morning, Jarrett stared at the changes

153

Chalky and his helpers had brought about. The windows were broken, and the wall below hacked into splinters. Thrust through the gap were half a dozen logs, while furniture had been piled against the lumber, along with the drapes from the window. The only clear floor space was a path between the door and the huge safe in the corner.

'You sure you're right about this?' Chalky asked.

'No, but I doubt if Vosper will be either. He won't take the risk,' Jarrett said, cocking his head as the sound of hoof beats reached him. 'Let's do it.'

Chalky struck a match and lit the torch. Flames blazed to the ceiling and he tossed the firebrand onto the drapes. The cloth ignited with a whoosh and within seconds the heap of furniture was alight. The two men backed out of the door, the pungent smell of smoke pursuing them.

'How many with him?' Chalky asked.

'Just two. The rest might be some time.'

Chalky grinned. 'We got a welcome ready.'

Jarrett glanced back. 'Hope we didn't set that alight too soon.'

'Don't think so,' Chalky said quietly. Framed in the doorway before them stood Durgan Vosper, pure hatred contorting his smooth features.

'I've got you now, Jarrett!' Vosper's dark eyes were alight with fury. 'You should have kept running while you had the chance.'

'This town's finished running,' Jarrett replied evenly. He stood aside so Vosper could see the smoke beginning to curl out through the open door of the room behind him.

'I lit a fire to welcome you home. Shame you don't trust banks.'

'What?' Vosper took a few steps forward, staring into the thickening smoke.

'I'd guess there's a lot of important paper locked up in that safe,' Jarrett said. 'Money's not enough, is it, Vosper. You own most of Harper's Mill, which means the land deeds are in there too.'

'They won't come to any harm inside the safe.'

Jarrett smiled. 'That's what the folks of New Jersey thought when their bank went up in flames three years back, but when they opened that big metal door all they found inside was ash.'

Doubt crept across Vosper's face. 'Damn you!' he said at last, starting forward.

'Fire ain't hot enough yet,' Chalky said, putting out a foot to trip him. As Vosper fell he flung out an arm, taking Jarrett down with him, and at that exact instant a rifle barked from the front door.

The bullet skimmed over Jarrett's head. His hands were moving to the familiar grip, sighting on his target even as he crashed to the floor. The Winchester barked and some-body cried out in pain. Amazingly fast for a man of his age and bulk, Chalky White crossed the intervening space to kick the gun out of Jude's hands. The youngster stared up at him through pain filled eyes.

'I said we should have killed you,' Chalky said, looking at the stain spreading across the youngster's belly. 'Dyin' of a gut shot's kinda slow an' painful boy.'

'Then finish me.' Jude ground the words out through gritted teeth, then another wave of pain hit him and he whimpered, tears starting from his eyes. 'It hurts. You gotta help me!'

Chalky picked up the youngster's gun and turned back to Jarrett. He was on his feet, watching Vosper as he stood at the door of the burning room, the flames roaring their menace as they crept ever closer. 'Don't you ever fight your own battles, Vosper?'

'Never found the need.' Vosper turned his head, a travesty of a smile on his lips. 'I hope you aren't afraid of fire, Jarrett.'

'What are you talkin' about?' Chalky trained Jude's rifle on Vosper.

'Look behind you.'

As one Jarrett and Chalky turned. At the end of the hall stood Zeke, one arm folded around Kate Sallis, the other holding a knife to her throat. The huge mill foreman grinned.

'Reckon you'll want to put down those guns down.'

Jarrett lowered the Winchester to the floor. Chalky White hesitated.

Vosper smiled, addressing himself to Jarrett. 'Did you really think I believed that story she concocted? You'd better tell the old man to get rid of that gun, unless you want your little lady to die.'

'Do as he says, Chalky.' Jarrett forced the words out as the knife pressed harder against Kate's throat. Reluctantly Chalky bent to lay the rifle down.

'Wise move.' Vosper's smile widened. 'Now you're going to fetch my belongings from the safe, Jarrett. Turn the dial to eight five four and pull the handle down. I'd advise you to be quick.'

Jarrett swallowed hard, the smoke harsh in his throat.

'Eight five four, Jarrett,' Vosper repeated softly. 'Bring out the money and the deed box and Zeke will let her go. She'll be on the *Fortune* when it leaves town, I promise.'

'Rick, no!' Kate screamed at him, struggling helplessly in Zeke's arms. The big man simply tightened his grip and bent his head to force his mouth over hers. He looked up afterwards, licking his lips and smiling at Jarrett.

'Cheated us out of that other piece of candy,' he said, 'be a real shame to slice this one up.'

'Rick!' Kate's despairing wail followed Jarrett as he ran into the inferno. He could see nothing through the smoke and the heat hit his body like a hammer blow. Ducking low he groped his way across the room, holding onto the breath he'd taken out in the hall, refusing to give in to his lungs' demand for more air. He made no move towards the safe, heading instead for the window where the fire was hottest, his arms raised to protect his face from the terrible heat.

Bright lights shot like lightning across his vision. Unable to hold out any longer without taking a breath he let air thick with smoke trickle into his mouth. Coughs racked him. He could smell his flesh beginning to scorch. Jarrett stumbled against something and almost fell. From its shape he guessed he'd found the cabinet that had stood against the wall beside the safe.

A sudden draught blew through the room and the roar of the flames intensified, but for a second the smoke parted and he could see the logs that had been dragged inside, flames devouring the resinous bark and turning the wood to white gold.

There was no time for thought. With a strength he never knew he possessed Jarrett picked up the cabinet and straightened his back. Crashing down onto the blazing logs it made a bridge across the flames for a split second, before the fire reached greedily for this new fodder. By then Jarrett was running up a sloping ramp that lurched wildly and threatened to tip him off. Three steps, four, the flames charring his boots, the legs of his pants catching light. Then with a wild leap he was out in the open and rolling in cool wet mud, over and over until he landed in a half frozen puddle. He lay there for a long moment, coughs racking his body.

At last Jarrett sat up. On the front of his right leg a patch of flesh the size of his fist looked like raw meat, and the backs of his hands were blistering, but that was the worst of it. He drew his .45 and limped cautiously to the side door where Zeke and Kate had entered. He stalked silent as a cat across the polished floor.

Zeke stood alongside Vosper, staring into the blaze, his arms still around Kate, but with the blade in his hand no longer pressing against her throat. She hung in the big man's arms unresisting, tears rolling silently down her cheeks, while Chalky White stood hesitating in the doorway of the burning room.

With cold deliberation Jarrett lifted the pistol. 'You're looking the wrong way,' he said. Zeke turned and threw up a hand as the bullet took him in the temple, then he dropped, dead before he hit the ground. Vosper spun in amazement as Kate pulled clear and ran to fling her arms around Jarrett.

Chalky White stared, a grin spreading across his face. 'Glad I didn't go in there after you, son,' he said.

Jarrett returned the smile. 'Be obliged if you'd take Kate back to town for me. Figure Annie and Mrs Capelli will take care of her.'

'No, wait.' Kate clung to him then released her hold as Jarrett winced. 'I'll go, but first I have to say I'm sorry, Rick. I was so wrong. I saw her. That poor little girl . . .' There were fresh tears in her eyes. 'I should have trusted you.'

He planted a kiss on her forehead, catching the sweet scent of her hair. 'I'll forgive you,' he said, 'on one condition.'

'Anything.'

'Next time I ask you, promise you'll say yes.'

Kate flushed and nodded. 'I promise.'

She turned to smile back at him as Chalky led her away.

Vosper hadn't moved. Jarrett fished beneath his belt and took out the badge. He went closer, holding it so Vosper could be in no doubt about the words it bore.

'I rode six years with Marty Sallis,' he said, 'before he

lost his arm and took to the Bible in place of a gun. Best partner a man could wish for, everything a US Marshal should be. Marty deserved better than to die with a bullet in his back. And you had him killed for a patch of mud.'

Vosper's dark eyes travelled from the gun in Jarrett's hand to the flames licking around the door frame. 'But I didn't tell Felipe to shoot him . . .'

'No? But you let him know the priest had become a problem, and that was enough. Then there was Greenwood and Westerman. You're a murderer, Vosper, several times over. You have to pay the price.' Jarrett faced him with a humourless smile. 'The people of Harper's Mill want their town back, don't reckon we'll have any trouble finding a jury.'

'It doesn't have to end that way.' A touch of panic sounded in Vosper's voice. 'There's a lot of money in that safe, Jarrett, it's yours. Just give me a chance.'

Jarrett nodded. 'Sure.' With a quick thrust of his boot he sent Jude's discarded rifle sliding into the blazing study.

'If you fetch the money you can keep it, all you have to do is shoot your way out, Vosper. Fight your own fight for once in your life.'

Vosper stared into Jarrett's implacable eyes, then without a word he turned and ran into the inferno. For a while there was only the crackle and roar of the voracious flames, then came a single agonized scream.

Jarrett returned the .45 to its holster. He picked up the Winchester from the floor and limped out of the burning mansion and down the hill to the town where Kate was waiting for him.